The Islamic family of **Zaynab Alkali** came from Dam, a village in Borno State, Nigeria — but they moved to a Christian village in Gongola State where **Zaynab Alkali** was brought up. She graduated from Bayero University, Kano, with a B.A. degree in English. She has taught at the universities of Bayero and Maiduguri. At present she is Senior Lecturer in English at the University of Maiduguri, Borno State.

*The Stillborn*, the first novel by Zaynab Alkali, reflects her belief that women throughout Africa should strive and be encouraged to fulfil their potential. Zaynab Alkali continues to write and her second novel *The Virtuous Woman* is also published by LONGMAN.

# THE STILLBORN

## Zaynab Alkali

with an introduction by
Dr Stuart Brown

Longman

Longman Group UK Limited,
Longman House, Burnt Mill, Harlow,
Essex CM20 2JE, England
and Associated Companies throughout the world.

© Zaynab Alkali 1988

First published 1984
First published as Longman African Classic 1989
Third impression 1990

Produced by Longman Group (FE) Ltd
Printed in Hong Kong

ISBN 0-582-02657-1

*Dedicated to my children:*
   *Yashuwa*
   *Fatima*
   *Baba Shettima*
   *Mama Habiba*
   *Hajja Amina*

# Introduction

## The Plot

Modernisation; the city and the village; the generation gap, polygamy; the role of women in times of social change . . . *The Stillborn* touches on several of the themes that dominate recent African fiction. The particular interest, and significance, of the novel is that it treats those concerns, especially the condition of women in contemporary Nigeria, from the *authentic* perspective of a woman brought up to accept the values and norms of a traditional society, albeit one that is, even when the story begins, under strain.

When the novel opens Li, the central character, is thirteen and returning to her village at the completion of her primary education (all the education that is considered appropriate for a girl in her community). The story takes us inside the family compound to help us understand the ritual and routine of rural life, the sources of tension within families and villages, and the pressures on the girls particularly to conform to established stereotypes of behaviour. Li is something of a rebel and breaks various taboos in her quest for self fulfilment. The novel charts her courtship, a marriage that is blighted by the betrayals of her husband Habu, and Li's determination to resist the pressures of society and create an independent career and future for herself.

In parallel with Li's story the novel follows the fate of two other women whose lives and dreams are similarly warped — *are stillborn* — by the brutality of a social order designed by and — ostensibly — in, the best interests of men. One, Li's elder sister Awa, accepts the role assigned her and passively becomes 'the mother of the house', or as Li describes her at the end of the novel, 'another who had given her life for the happiness of others'. The other, Li's best school-friend Faku, is a victim of the city; mistreated by her husband and tormented by her in-laws because she has only one child, Faku tries to escape but, as far as her society is concerned, that can only mean that she has accepted the one traditional role for an independent woman, that of prostitution.

*The Stillborn* is not simply a Feminist novel transposed to an African setting. The social analysis is more complex, more aware of the real traumas that the modernisation process in Nigeria is causing. Zaynab Alkali understands that many men, too, suffer from the stereotyped life routes that traditional society imposes and several male characters in *The Stillborn* are victims of the tension between traditional attitudes and modern realities.

The novel closes, teasingly for those who would insist on a crude Feminist analysis, with Li, at thirty-three, having accomplished many of her ambitions — 'she was a successful teacher and the owner of a huge modern and enviable building'. She feels that her struggle to assert her economic independence is only valid if it is a means to an end. She wants to be able to establish a relationship with her husband based on the understanding of their being equal partners and not on the traditional master-dependent relationship that has so badly soured their first attempt at married life. Li has just nursed her grandfather, Kaka, — the symbol of tradition in the novel — in his final illness, and with his death she feels free to break the last taboo and return to the city, alone, to search out Habu and try to re-establish their relationship, but on *her* terms.

## Setting

Although Zaynab Alkali's family belonged to the devoutly Muslim Tura group of the Kanuri people in what is now Borno State in northern Nigeria, her father moved the family to the mainly Christian village of Garkida, in what is now Gongola state, shortly before she was born. So Zaynab Alkali spent the first ten years of her life — before beginning her formal education — in that traditionally structured but culturally diverse environment. That background is an important key to the setting of *The Stillborn*, for although the novel is not autobiographical in terms of the events it chronicles — Li's struggles and discoveries are very far from the academic and personal success that Mrs Alkali has enjoyed. Much of the power of the novel grows from the finely observed re-creation of a culturally and religiously 'mixed' village, somewhere in northern Nigeria, in the late colonial period.

Indeed the village might be said to be the dominant 'personality' in the novel; its traditions, rituals and economic well-being setting the social and cultural horizons of its members. The village is never named, it is always 'the village', an anonymity that suggests an idea of 'home', that is both archetypal and immemorial. In *The Stillborn* as in many other African novels that focus on the issue of modernisation, the village is a symbol of the past, the stage of the ancestors, the tap-root of collective and individual identity. Li's village — for all its petty spites and feuding — is presented as an oasis of order, where individual's roles are clearly defined by sex, age and custom and where fortune or disaster depend on the whim of the gods.

The old gods that watch over Li's village are housed in a cave in the woods nearby — Kaka worships them still and they retain their potency, as metaphor anyway, for the younger members of the community too. But if the old gods do watch over the village, already, when the novel begins, the outside world has impinged on their domain. The Hill Station and the Mission Memorial Hospital are a strong presence in the village. For although, ironically perhaps, 'it lent its light to those two places only', the intrusive hum of the electricity generator is the background against which the 'rustic' voices of the villagers must be heard.

Zaynab Alkali vividly re-creates the life and atmosphere of the village; its routines, its rituals and its people. It is in the descriptions of its domestic ritual, its markets and its festivals that we get a real sense of the life of the village. The account of the Tuesday market during harmattan (p.28) is particularly effective; the dusty, hustling cacophany of the market place alive with drumming, the begging madman and raucous naked children is brilliantly observed.

> The road to the market suddenly seemed to spring into life. Already a few commercial lorries had arrived from some neighbouring villages, bringing goods from the cities. Women, bent almost double under their loads, walked slowly and answered greetings with a wave of the hand. Donkey owners, with mouths muffled under headcovers, swore and beat their

animals. Naked children, their bellies protruding and shining from the early beancake, chased and shouted at each other.

Once inside the market Li took her time and walked slowly, absorbing the early morning scene. The dust increased as stalls were swept. A few people wet the ground to damp down the dust. Li wove her way through the growing din as greetings were exchanged and haggling began. The Kalangu drummers, stationed behind the meatsellers, beat their drums with extra vigour to ward off the cold. A madman, holding a dirty pan, went round the food stalls dancing to the rhythm of the drums and raising more dust in his frenzy. As he moved towards a beancake stall, a fat woman got up angrily and chased him away from her stall.

Elsewhere the almost incidental descriptions of the way people work, and the accounts of the 'cultural dances' that are held to celebrate the full moon or to mark a death, suggest the texture of village life. Indeed the occasions which those 'cultural dances' provide for the young people to meet become the moments when 'things happen' in the novel, when promises are made and decisions taken. The 'news' of those decisions is transmitted to the community as a whole — and sometimes to the reader — through the informal meetings of the older members of the village. The gatherings of gossiping, complaining, plotting villagers become a kind of tragi-comic chorus, relishing bad news and embroidering small grievances into serious accusations. Significantly, it is a chorus led by the deformed, impotent Manu.

The positive side of community life is seen, though, especially when Li is finally preparing to leave the village for her husband's house in the city,

The news of her journey had already spread in the village. People would stop her on the way to ask when she was leaving and what job her husband did in the city. They would then fish into their pockets or untie their wrapper and bring out money ranging from two

pence to two shillings — to aid her on her journey.
(p.67)

Others contribute various food items and household utensils until the bulk of her possessions becomes too large for her inlaws to carry. When they complain that many of the items are unnecessary in the city the old women insist that

> Their daughter would be in a strange city among strange people. Who would lend her anything to use?
> (p.67)

That episode serves as a metaphor for the incomprehension that characterises the conflict between rural and urban life in the novel, the villagers cannot *imagine* the kind of lives people live in the city, the city folk cannot *remember* how different the world seemed when the village was all they knew. The food and utensils that had been a source of pride and status in the village become a cause of humiliation as Li gets closer to the city.

The city itself hardly appears in *The Stillborn*, though its influence is at the heart of the events the novel chronicles. Li seems hardly to venture out of her compound, Habu and Garba's city is a threatening, destructive place. The villagers construct their own myth of the city that is at once nightmarish but is also a place of opportunity. When Audu, one of the 'chorus', complains of insomnia caused by worry Manu accuses him of exaggeration — 'People with sons in the big city have no problems' he asserts. Audu responds by telling the story of his son's emasculation by the topsy-turvey values of the city — 'like a woman, he cooks for the big men'.

Awa, wise before her time in the early part of the novel, feels no need to leave her home village to visit the city because, she predicts, soon enough 'the city will come to us'. By the end of the novel, when Li returns for her grandfather's funeral, that prediction has come true.

> The main street was lighted by the numerous kerosene lamps and mini gas generators from the rich houses. She moved slowly among the throng of busy people hawkers of all kinds of wares, idlers and street-walkers.

On each side of the street, shops, kiosks and stalls were springing up. Li also observed with sadness that the front yards of elders and ward heads, that used to serve as recreation centres for yelling children were now commercial centres for petty traders. The days of dancing, singing and holding hands under the watchful eyes of the full moon were over.

## Characters

To a great extent *The Stillborn* is an extended portrait of a single character, Li. The other characters are seen against her, as it were, and serve to point up themes and issues that Li's story touches on. But Li is not a fixed, fully formed personality, we see her gradually growing into herself; the novel spans some twenty years (seventy years if you include Li's final dream) and the way Li's character develops through that period is both a major theme in the novel and the armature around which it is structured.

When the novel opens Li is thirteen, 'five feet four, with skin the colour of brown earth, a graceful neck and a slender body', with large, penetrating eyes. She is a lively, impetuous, self confident girl, qualities which her parents would call rude, wilful and stubborn. She is soon bored by the restictive nature of life in the compound, resenting her father's petty tyranies. It is not village life itself that she rails against at first, but rather that her father is too much of a religious zealot and scorns the traditional 'cultural' activities of the village which at least allowed the young people to meet and mix. So Li must contrive ways to attend those 'forbidden' social events.

For all her rebelliousness and independence of mind however, Li is always and fundamentally a 'daughter of the village'. She is trained in its traditions and values, even down to retaining its superstitions — when a chameleon crosses her path for instance (p.95) or she hears an owl's cry in the night. (p.65) All the same, Li had always been somehow 'different', even her strange and difficult birth (pp.4-7) seeming to portend some quirk of personality. She is a *dreamer* in both senses of the word; at one level she is materially ambitious, unwilling to accept the role fate offers her, and she aspires to a very different kind of life, in the city;

> A place where she would have an easy life, free from
> slimey calabashes and evil smelling goats. She looked
> down at her coarse hands and feet. One of these days
> she would be a different woman, with polished nails
> and silky shining hair. (p.55)

And at another level she is subject to dreams which predict
future events, which guide and guard her. The first of these,
when, as an eleven year old she had a frightening dream that
foretold the accident at the prayer meeting in which Baba was
injured, marked a turning point in her relationship with her
father. He had refused to listen to her warning, regarding such
a vision as evidence of an 'evil streak' in her personality. (Like
several other women in their story Li's 'strangeness' means that
she risks being thought of as a witch.) After the prediction came
true Baba had become uncomfortable in her presence and
avoided her. For Li, who until then had 'hung on his words
as the ultimate truth', the events shows her up as a fallible and
bigoted man.

Li's sense of isolation is compounded by the cold and rather
distant relationship she has with her mother. Unable to
understand her submissive attitude to Baba and his 'discipline',
Li can never confide in her mother in the way that Faku can
in hers. Li's mother is a shadowy character who hardly features
in the plot of the novel at all. She is herself something of an
outsider, having been married by Baba as a 'heathen' — a
fact he constantly refers to as their relationship becomes more
strained. Only much later in the novel, after her own marriage
has gone wrong, does Li begin to appreciate her mother's
difficulties and to admire her independence of spirit. It is the
produce of *her* farm which keeps the family fed in the years
of Baba's illness and Dan Fiama's decline into alcholism.
Perhaps, as Baba says, 'the lion cub takes after its mother'
and Li's patience and determination is an inheritance from
her mother.

As a young woman Li is outspoken and always does things
'in a rush'. When Habu approaches the two sisters at the dance,
Awa's reaction is to shun him; Li, on the other hand, welcomes
his attention, and is charmed by his bold 'style'. Soon she is
dreaming of their future together in the city and planning her

escape from the confines of family and village. Here the two dominant elements of her personality — the capacity to dream and the determination to achieve particular ends — come together. A third element, patience, is acquired the hard way, as her dream shatters and she waits the four long years for Habu to send for her from the city.

The rest of Li's married life is a series of trials; she must adapt to the city and the 'new', resentful Habu she finds there, she must learn to be a mother and she must find new resources of patience as she is again abandoned to the village. The positive side of this experience though is that Li learns to count her blessings rather than dwell on her misfortunes, Hajia — her childless landlady and only confidant in the city — teaches her that, and so, in different ways do Faku and Awa. Li sees that she must resist the role of *victim* that is the woman's traditional lot if she is to make the most of her potential. The vehemence with which the women of the village regard her when — because she is thought to be flirting with their husbands — she becomes a threat to their marriages, and thus to their status, their very identity, reinforces Li's determination to escape that traditional role. (p.85) But it is finally the impoverished state of her family's compound, with Baba dead, Sule in exile, Awa's husband Dan Fiama become an alchoholic and Habu seemingly indifferent, that stirs Li to ignore the social stigma and return to the city, unaccompanied, to work and study for the qualifications that will give her independence. Ironically perhaps, she has opted to become 'the man of the house'.

The Li who inhabits the final scenes of the novel; mature, tolerant, worldly-wise, established as a successful woman in her own right, and willing to risk further rebuffs in order to fulfill at least part of her childhood dream, has come a long way from the naive, impulsive schoolgirl she was when the novel opens. That journey towards a kind of liberation, of *self* determination, is the essence of Zaynab Alkali's purpose in *The Stillborn*.

As I remarked above most of the other characters in the story serve as pointers to aspects of Li's personality rather than as fully formed individuals in their own right, but it is worth looking at some of them briefly here for the issues their stories raise. It is apparent that the male figures, with the exception perhaps of Kaka, are weak and isolated victims of circumstance. The women on the other hand, though they suffer and seem oppressed by the ways in which their societies are organised, support each other and seem, when the novel closes, to have emerged from what Li's calls their common 'struggle to survive' with more success.

## Baba, Kaka and Grandma

Baba is a stern, sickly, unsympathetic character, possessed by a 'mad obsession with discipline'. His own childhood had been far from idlyic, his mother died when he was six and his step-mother, Li's outrageous 'grandmother', cast a shadow over his youth. The difficult relationship with his own parents mirrors Li and Sule's conflicts with him. (The 'generation gap' is a minor theme in the novel, part of the larger disruption that is 'modernisation'.) A convert himself and so, perhaps, uncertain of his own status, Baba trys to instil the fundamentals of his new faith into his reluctant children. Kaka, his father, puts Baba's failure in human terms down to 'the quest for modern living coupled with a foreign culture'. Certainly Baba is trapped between worlds — unable to identify fully with either the tradition of his father or the demands of his new religion and the culture it implies.

Kaka himself is an old man when the story opens and, at the time of his death, twenty years later, is truely 'the ancient one' . . 'the last of his kind'. Kaka never accepted his son's — or his people's — conversion to European ways and values. So he lives a secret life, visiting the herbalist — rather than the mission hospital — when sick, worshipping the old gods and offering sacrifices to them in the cave behind the Hill Station. He is especially fond of Li because she reminds him of his own mother, but also because he admires her spirit. Their special relationship means that he can restrain young Li when Baba and his 'discipline' no longer bother her.

Kaka's relationship with his wife is, at best, tense, but they are in many ways, similar personalities. A 'shrewd, dominating' figure, a self proclaimed priestess of the old religion, grandma is an independent woman in a society that cannot accommodate her. A great beauty in her youth — married fourteen times she claims — she had refused Kaka's attempts to divorce her, 'drove three other wives from the compound' and generally gets her own way. She is scornful of Kaka, Baba and, it seems, all the men of the village — she no longer needs them. To that extent grandma provides another model for Li, who, late in the novel, argues that life has taught her, too, that a woman need not depend on men but should rather rely on her own efforts and resources. That there is scope for Li to achieve that ambition says something about the way the process of social change has, in some ways, opened up possibilities for women that didn't exist when grandma was young. The respective fates of the two old people is revealing, too — whereas grandma becomes a kind of evil presence lurking in the compound, Kaka becomes a respected figure, the father of the village. But nevertheless Kaka's values die with him, and insofar as he attempts to stem the tide of 'moderisation' his rearguard action must finally be counted a failure.

## Sule, Habu, Dan Fiama and Garba

Sule's first words in the novel are, 'Its a rotten life!' and for most of the story fate seems determined to prove him right. Not only his own experience but that of his whole generation seems cursed. It is they who must actually go out and carve new life routes through the contradictions of the new society; but their tradition has not equipped them to do this. The story of Sule's life in exile abroad, (pp. 97-8) when he is rescued from the brink of ruin by a stranger who trusts him and acts towards him like the kind of father he 'never had before', develops the theme of escape and rescue that runs through the novel and says something about the failure of his own community to provide a channel for his talent and energy.

Habu's 'escape' from the village leads only to disaster, however, and until Li's plan to 'rescue' him is uncovered, it seems he has no 'friend' to aid him. Habu is a tragic figure, although he seems at first a hero and then a villain. His life begins to go wrong when he arrives in the city and becomes entangled in its unruly ways. Unable to extricate himself from his relationship with his 'city wife' he cannot explain either his predicament or his feelings to Li, and so his frustration breeds on itself. His final tragedy comes when he is involved in a car accident; left crippled and so unable to provide for his city wife, she too abandons him. Habu is a victim; of his tradition, which imposes it own norms of masculinity on him so that he is unable to express his true feelings, of the city which confuses and ensnares him, and in a way of the gradual liberation of the women in his life who assert their own independence at his expense.

Dan Fiama and Garba are 'victims' too, victims of changes in their society which they can't comprehend and over which they have no control. As a young man Dan Fiama is held up as an example to others by the village elders, 'a good mallam and a good farmer'. (p.49) He is also the headmaster — 'H.M.' — of the village school, where Awa is a teacher. His moral and intellectual horizons are set by the tradition which also gives him status. That, in the end, is his tragedy. For as the village is overtaken by the city so Dan Fiama's status is undermined. He does not become the headmaster of the new school, his qualifications and experience equip him for only a very low level position in the new social order. His pride broken, but without any real alternative except to stay on and endure his humiliation, Dan Fiama turns to drink as a way of blocking out the world he cannot cope with. Although he continues to father children he neglects his duties to his family and at the end of the novel he is a figure of scorn in the village where once he had been held up as a model.

Garba is also a 'son of the soil' but has had a very different life. Brought up in the city by his prostitute mother, he has returned to the village on the death of his father, a waster who left many debts. Garba roars about the village on his motorbike, 'reckless', lazy and irreverent. The opinion of the 'chorus' is that he is a dangerous and undesirable character. But for Faku he seems to offer a chance to escape from the struggle of her life in the village and is keen to return with him to 'civilisation', as he puts it. But his business there is shadowy and insecure, and he soon gives Faku cause to lament her 'escape'. Lacking any sympathy for Faku's plight Garba connives at her gradual estrangement. When she leaves he feels slighted, but is powerless to do anything about it. For all his boasting about the possibilities the city offers he has not prospered there; already in his fifties by the end of the novel, his dreams, too, prove stillborn.

## Awa and Faku

Awa and Faku are in many ways similar characters, but the choices they make, and the men they attach themselves to, mean that their lives diverge to form the poles of experience between which Li struggles to plot a middle way.

When the story begins Awa is a passive, level headed girl who seems to relish the traditional roles set out for a woman in her village. She aspires only to become a respectable wife and mother. Her meek, subservient attitude to Baba is contrasted with Li's rebelliousness. But, unmarried at eighteen, Awa already fears that she is destined to become an 'old maid'. Unlike Li she has no hankering after the city and its sophisticated ways, her only mildly contentious opinion seems to be that she dislikes polygamy, not on any feminist grounds but rather because it causes domestic tensions and aggravations within the family compound. When she becomes Dan Fiama's wife it seems her 'goodness' has been rewarded — he is regarded as a prize catch. But events change her man and although she dutifully produces a child every year, they are fathered, as she puts it in a moment of bitterness, by 'the chief alcoholic'. Awa has to provide for her growing family somehow as well as bring them up. Within her tradition she has no real redress, she is doing what she is supposed to. Dan Fiama can break down, abandon his duties and responsibilities, but she, as the woman, *must* cope.

Yet, despite her grim personal experience Awa remains a champion of that traditional role. When Li returns to the compound and tells her the story of Habu's betrayal Awa urges her sister to marry the rich but unprincipled Alhaji Bature because, she argues, 'every woman needs a man, if only to mend the fence.' (p.88) Perhaps Awa is unable to see any better alternatives — Li's assertiveness and quest for independence has not exactly brought her joy and Faku's fate — seemingly driven to prostitution — seems worse.

Tragedy haunts Faku's life; her father died when she was six and then her two brothers were killed in a freak accident. Such ill fortune is seen by the villagers as evidence that the family is cursed and Faku's mother is branded as a witch. It is easy to understand, then, why she is attracted to Garba and the prospect of escape from the drudgery of her life in the village.

So Faku gladly becomes Garba's second wife, for, unlike Awa, she has no particular objection to polygamy. Marriage offers her a kind of independence, and if her housband 'could afford to feed a dozen other wives', she argued, 'who was she to object?' The reality of a polygamous household proves to be rather different, however, especially for a wife who seems unable to 'give' her husband many children. Although she has one child Faku's relationship with Garba quickly sours; her co-wife — 'the mother of the house' who has nine children by him, resents her presence and plots against her. Faku's life in the city becomes as unhappy as her village life had been, but when she finally makes the break with Garba she cannot bring herself to return to her mother's compound.

Garba and the villagers assume that Faku has taken to prostitution, but when she re-appears at the end of the story she seems, no matter what depths she has been driven to in order to survive in the intervening years, to have finally landed on her feet. Supported by an older, more experienced woman — just as Li is supported by Hajia and Awa by her long suffering mother — Faku is working towards a post as a social welfare officer, a role her life's hard road has equipped her for very well.

## Themes and Imagery

The two major and inextricably interwoven themes that run through *The Stillborn* are, as I've said, familiar concerns of recent Nigerian fiction; the tensions caused by 'modernisation' and the place of women in Nigerian society.

Both 'modernisation' and 'tradition' are loaded and contentious concepts in this context. Many would argue that they are set up in a false opposition, that so called 'traditional societies' in west Africa were never static, but were always in a state of change, of gradual adaptation to new climatic, technological, political and cultural circumstances. Always involved, that is, in a modernisation process. 'Gradual' is the key word though; over time societies evolve to accommodate changed circumstances, and even when quite drastic changes are involved as a result of conquest or natural disasters, some cultural fundamentals remain to structure the new society, traditions like the respect for age and ancestors, the respective roles and status of men and women, attitudes to land, etc. What is meant by 'modernisation' in recent Nigerian fiction is the acceleration of that process of adaptation — and the disruption that follows in its wake — by the incursion of technology and material goods and the Western cultural values that go with them, into rural, *relatively* stable and established communities. In *The Stillborn* these changes are perceived as *city* ways, because, naturally enough, they appear and are established first of all in the cities. Various aspects of this theme are focussed in the experiences of different characters; in the cultural unease of Baba, the despair of Kaka and in the ordeals of Habu, Sule and Dan Fiama. In her final analysis of that confrontation between village and city, Li judges that although it seems to offer possibilities of escape, the city 'destroys dreams'. It is the most damning thing she could say, especially when we see that, by the end of the novel, the city has effectively *consumed* the village.

The status of women in contemporary Nigeria is explored through the experiences of all the female characters in the story and links with many of the issues brought up by the 'modernisation' theme. The lives of the minor characters point up particular issues; the passing debate over polygamy, focussed in Faku's story (and the story of her co-wife), is an issue that is particularly relevant in northern Nigeria now. The importance of potency and fertility is also touched on in Faku's story but is brought out particularly in the stories of Hajia, Li's landlady (pp.72-3), and Manu's bride (pp.53-4). And the vulnerability of women, their dependence on the men with whom they are entangled, is poignantly sketched in the story of Habu's mistress (pp.92-3). But it is the experience of Li and the other major female characters that is at the heart of Zaynab Alkali's 'argument'. Insofar as it can be reduced to a simple 'statement' *The Stillborn* seems to offer a prescription for self-assertion and self-help. Li and the other women who come through are characters who struggle and grow and support one another; although her original naive dreams are *stillborn* Li is constantly striving to make new dreams come true.

Dreams are an important element in the structuring of the story for they show Li — and the reader — pictures of the future and their occurrence always marks a turning point in the plot. I have mentioned the first dream and the effect that had on

Li's relationship with Baba. Later Li has dreams that foretell her father's death (pp.73-4) and comprehend the extent of Faku's suffering with Garba and the city (pp.79-80). Most significant is Li's dream of her own future that occurs right at the end of the novel. After nursing Kaka into his last dream Li has a dream of her own great-granddaughter's wedding, fifty years into the future. Close to death herself, Li advises the girl to make the most of her opportunities, not to waste *her* life on empty dreaming.

> It is well to dream child . . . Everybody does, and as
> long as we live, we shall continue to dream. But it
> is also important to remember that like babies dreams
> are conceived but not all dreams are born alive. Some
> are aborted. Others are stillborn. ( p.104)

In the dream the old woman who is Li speaks of the frustrations she has endured, but she speaks also of her deep affection for Habù. When she awakes Li recalls the dream and knows that 'the bond that had tied her to the father of her child was not ruptured' (p.105) It is that certainty that guides Li to go and search for Habu in the city; she would not let that childhood dream of their life together be aborted by the circumstances of the intervening years, most of her life is ahead of her and she determines to make the best of it.

That Li is a *dreamer* is important to our understanding of how and why she succeeds against the odds while others are beaten down by the social order they must live in. Her dreams set her apart from the others, confirm the 'strangeness' that was apparent even in the manner of her birth; her dreaming makes her vulnerable — what she sees in her dreams is not always pleasant, — but her ability to dream, and her insistence that dreams offer important messages from the unconscious, not just, as Baba claims, shadows of 'what you think about during the day', gives her a strength, a confidence, to attempt what others will not dare.

Stewart Brown
Centre of West African Studies
University of Birmingham.

# Chapter One

The lorry swerved from side to side and Li held to the sides of the bench. She felt sick and, closing her eyes for a moment, softly uttered a prayer. Nervously, she cast a glance at the others, who were fellow pupils going home for the end of the year holidays. None of them seemed to have noticed the reckless speed at which they were going. They were happy children, singing and clapping in rhythm to the droning of the engine, and calling praise-names to the lorry driver who would from time to time accelerate in acknowledgement. Li felt alone, although she was among friends and age-mates, none of whom was much older than herself.

The clapping and singing continued endlessly amid the heat, the dust and the reckless speed.

'My God,' Li swore softly to herself, looking round the crowded and disorganised lorry. 'Something must be wrong with me.'

Feeling numb in both legs, she tried to ease them, but could not. Something or someone was sitting on them. She gave up trying and forced her mind to more pleasant things. She, too, was happy to be going home after completing her primary seven in a neighbouring village. The thought of seeing her numerous brothers and sisters made her want to clap and sing with the others. For a moment she thought of her parents and a dark shadow crossed her mind, threatening to dampen her happiness. She quickly warded it off. This was no time to indulge in unhappy thoughts.

The lorry swerved dangerously once more as it took a sharp turn and the occupants were thrown to one side. The singing turned to shrieks and Li muttered what she thought was her last prayer. Suddenly the weight shifted from her legs.

'Thank God for that,' she thought. 'At least my legs are free.'

The shrieks died down immediately and several voices shouted that the village was in sight. Thirteen-year-old Faku, Li's closest friend, jumped up and, grabbing Li by the arm, shouted above the din:

'Climb the bench fast! We're almost there!' Li needed no

urging, if she were to avoid being buried under dusty pairs of shorts and sundry other garments. Everybody was up and clearing the dust from their eyes—just enough to see—as a dusty appearance was a respectable sign of having come from a faraway land. Li climbed the bench gingerly, holding onto the wooden bar for support. She could feel the blood returning to her feet and stamped them vigorously to encourage the flow. The lorry slowed down as it drew near the village. The scenery in front of them was spectacular.

From the distance of a few miles, and standing on a higher plane, they could take in the whole landscape at a glance. The village was large and unequally cleft in two by a long narrow stream, almost hidden by its bushy banks. The smaller side of the village was less crowded. It consisted of farmland and a few scattered mud huts which appeared quiet and deserted.

On the opposite and larger side, however, flourished a long stretch of fruit trees, richly dressed in green. Further down, the village lay sprawled in clusters of thatched mud huts. The sun's reflection on the few zinc roofs that were scattered among the clusters threw a blinding light across the village. Lengthwise the village extended out of sight, but its breadth ended with a range of hills. At the base of the hills was the European quarters known as the Hill Station. The houses here were built of stones and roofed with asbestos. Built on a much higher plane and facing the rest of the village, they had assumed the look of an overlord. This advantageous position was further heightened by a thick overgrowth of trees that shrouded the houses, giving them the desired privacy.

Li relived the village she knew so well at night. It was always calm and quiet. Only the sound of the mission generator could be heard. Situated between the Hill Station and the Memorial Hospital, it lent its light to these two places only. A visitor at night was apt to think that only these two places existed in the village. At exactly ten o'clock, the sound of the generator that had kept up a regular beating to the rhythm of the heartbeat of every child born for that generation, would die down, signalling the hour of sleep and releasing the night to the walking witches and discontented spirits. The same generator would usher in the beginning of a new day at exactly six in the morning.

After a few weeks at home, Li began to find the atmosphere in her father's compound suffocating. She felt trapped and unhappy. Already, she missed the kind of life she had lived at the primary boarding school, free and gay. At home the little ones were too young to understand the restrictions and the older ones too dull to react. They all seemed to accept the situation as natural except, of course, Sule, her senior brother, who suffered the silence with her. Restless and dissatisfied at home, the two got the worst treatment. Li and Sule minded very much the rules they considered stupid and unnecessarily rigid. They abhorred the 'don'ts' that heavily out-numbered the 'do's'.

'It's worse than a prison,' Li complained one day as she sat with her brothers and sisters in the cooking hut. Awa looked at her sullenly and shook her head. At eighteen she was the oldest child in the family, five years older than Li. Still unmarried, she shouldered half the responsibility of the house. Having completed class seven at primary school two years ago, Awa had remained at home as a teacher in the village primary school.

'Li, you have nothing to complain about,' Awa retorted. 'Would you rather be in one of the heathen homes?' To Awa's utter amazement, Li roared with laughter and Sule joined in.

'What are you laughing about?' Awa asked, insulted.

'Oh! Big sister, you kill us with laughter,' Li replied, wiping her eyes with the end of her wrapper. 'Those people you call heathens may not have embraced anybody's religion but they have their own ancestral gods.'

'Don't talk like that, Li. Are you also a heathen?' Awa demanded.

'Let me be a heathen,' Li said more seriously. 'I'd be much happier. At least I could go ease myself without having someone breathing down my neck demanding to know where I have been to.' She was silent for a while, staring at the fire that glowed in the hearth.

'What kind of life is this anyway? And you, big sister, so content with it.'

'It is a rotten life!' Sule interjected.

'Don't talk like that, Sule,' Awa warned.

'Yes, it is a rotten life,' Sule insisted. 'Look at you, eighteen years old, still at home, single. Not allowed to go out at all except to the market, the riverside, the prayer house and the school. Even then you are always watched. I tell you, if this continues, ten years from now you'll still be right here performing the same chores; fetching water and teaching a group of dirty children. Not to talk of being bossed by a cruel headmaster at school and an irate father at home. The only difference will be, you'll be ten years older and much more frustrated.'

'No, God knows, life should be better than this,' Li joined in. 'As for me, big brother, I can't wait to get out of this hell.'

The hut was suddenly plunged into silence. The smaller children looked from one face to another. Nobody could understand the extent of their feelings.

'Now wait,' Awa said as an afterthought. 'Dan Fiama, the headmaster, isn't cruel.' Li raised her eyebrows in mock horror and Sule burst into laughter.

'Since when did you discover that?' he asked, and that evoked general laughter in the hut. Awa turned her face away from them, obviously embarrassed.

'You know the trouble with you two,' Awa began, trying to skip the point about the headmaster. 'You are impatient and stubborn. You always have been, Li. Can't you remember what Mama said about your birth?' she asked, smiling mischievously.

'Oh no,' Li thought, not again.' She had heard that tale so many times and each time it was told there were considerable variations, depending on who told it. She was beginning to doubt its authencity.

'Mama was grinding some guinea corn when the labour pains started,' Awa began, looking round the faces that were now listening with rapt attention.

'No, it wasn't guinea corn, it was millet,' Sani, popularly known as Hitla, put in.

'Shut your mouth, Hitla,' said Becki Hirwa. 'You weren't born then.'

'Neither were you,' Sani countered. 'I thought you were two years later.'

'And you,' Hirwa added, 'four.'

'Uhmm,' Li grunted. 'Some story you have there.'

'Now you be silent, all of you,' Awa shouted. 'I don't need help from anybody. As Mama was grinding guinea corn,' she resumed, 'or whatever it was, she suddenly felt the urge to bear down. "Ah", she thought, "my stomach is playing tricks again".' Awa smiled knowingly. 'You know, she thought it was the usual call to the back yard and rushed to the pit. Ya! She nearly had Li down there!' With the last word, Awa opened her eyes wide in mock horror. The rest burst into fits of laughter.

'Wait,' Sani exclaimed, 'you should have been named "Timbili", the pitwoman.'

'Be silent, crooked nose, or I'll teach you how to respect your elders!' Li shouted.

'Elders? Who is talking about age? God bless Yakumba's patience. She is the oldest woman in the village and yet she allows people to talk. I wonder. . .'

'Enough of that, Sani. I have not finished yet,' Awa cut in impatiently. 'Li came tumbling out with the bag of waters intact.'

'Then the Hausas would have named her "Mairiga",' Sule said.

'You too, son-of-the-chief,' Li said eyeing him. 'Why, you should have called me that. I thought you were there when it happened.'

'No, I wasn't,' Sule replied.

'Yes, you were,' Li insisted. 'Holding onto ma's wrapper and screaming your head off at the same time.'

The rest giggled. They were warming to the show. A rare show indeed. Sule and Li seldom quarrelled. More often than not, they teamed up against the rest.

'Li isn't a bad name,' Sule said in an attempt to make up.

'Li wasn't the name I was given at birth. My real name is Mwapu, the fair one. And you all know that.'

'Well, you have grandmother to thank for the false one,' said Sule.

'What does Li mean then?' Sani asked, his eyes burning with curiosity.

Sule and Awa exchanged amused looks. Li shot him an angry glance.

'I know what it means! It is short for Libira—needle. Ma

always says your buttocks are as sharp as a needle. That's why you can never stay in one place for long.'

Li got up in a flash and kicked Sani on the shin. Sani howled with pain. Limping, he made for Li, fists clenched and eyes blazing. Awa saw that a fight was imminent and cut in quickly.

'Anybody who interrupts me again will be driven out into the cold. Now, I was saying that. . .'

'Belly full of worms,' Li growled, still fuming. Awa ignored the interruption.

'Li came with the bag of waters intact, but what frightened Mama so much was that she did not cry at birth.' The hut was silent. Everybody seemed to savour the piece of information.

'Well, big sister,' Li inclined her head to one side. 'I had no reason to cry. Why should I? Just to keep a tradition?'

'At birth a baby always cries. This is nature's way of heralding a newborn. You must be the odd one out not to adhere to this all-important tradition.'

'Maybe I cried. Who can swear I did not?'

'You mean, Li, you are doubting ma's report?'

'Now, big sister, keep ma out of this. She told the original tale, but you made the rest up,' Li replied.

'Well, forget the crying part of the story,' Awa replied, 'at least we had only her word for it. But what about the rest, Li—your hair, ears, and eyes?'

'What abut them? Were they missing?' Li said mockingly.

'It would have been more natural if they were. Your hair was as kinky as an adult's and your eyes were like old Yakumba's.' The children roared with laughter. 'As for your ears,' Awa strove to be heard above the din, 'Mama was wondering if you had holes in them at all. They were rolled up like banana shoots.' That set the rest roaring once more. 'Mama had to cover her head and ears until you were nine months old. I can still remember that clearly. Ask Kaka if you don't believe me.' Kaka was the father of their father.

'And my eyes, what did they do with them, tape them shut?' Li asked half mischievously, half with curiosity.

'There was nothing she could do with your eyes. Your plump face took care of that.'

'Why all the trouble?' Li asked.

'Mainly to save the visitors and the family from embarrass-ment. They kept on exclaiming and making embarrassed apologies when they saw you. In truth many people didn't know how to react, just because they thought you were some kind of monster,' Awa explained.

'Poor Mama, what a lot of trouble on her part for nothing. She should have known that I, Li, was no ordinary child. Why? Those were pure signs of a super-being,' Li boasted.

'Nonsense,' retorted Awa. 'Those were stubborn streaks.'

'Li is right you know, big sister.' Sule tried to worm his way back into Li's favour. 'Li is extraordinary. At least she looks like a river goddess.'

'Yes,' Sani cried, 'with the head of a woman and the tail of a fish.'

The smaller ones giggled, but Li ignored them completely and said, 'Well, they should have known better than to bridle me. I was born with my stubbornness.'

They heard Mama's unmistakable footsteps and stopped talking. Not that it mattered very much, as Mama was hard of hearing.

'Awa!' she called from the doorway. 'Go and fetch some water. Li, wash the dishes. Sani, take the sheep and goats to the hills to feed. Becki Hirwa, sweep the compound. The rest of you. . .'

By now they had dispersed to their various chores, leaving her standing alone in the doorway. It was a routine instruc-tion and never varied. Always the same words in the same order. 'What monotony,' Li thought. Even Mama's step as she walked away was mechanical.

Li shot out of the hut like an arrow. She always did things in a rush. Gathering the dishes, she set to work, humming to herself. Awa took a tin container and, retrieving her rub-ber slippers from under Mama's wooden bed, she slipped out quietly. The riverside was two miles away. Baba, their father, had instructed Mama never to send Li to fetch water. Awa was to go while Li did the dishes. This was because Li had always visited friends on her way to the riverside. At first Li had protested loudly at the arrangement but no one had lis-tened to her. She hated washing dishes and tried various ways of getting out of the ordeal, but all tricks failed.

Baba came out of his hut carrying a folding chair and a 'Teach yourself how to read' book. He stood for a minute and surveyed the compound as a farmer would his farm. His compound was big, maybe only second in size to the chief of the village. It was divided into three parts and his hut stood in the middle. If you were standing in front of his hut to your left would be Kaka's portion, which consisted of two huts. To your right would be Mama's portion, consisting of three huts, two belonging to the children. In Baba's position, in front of his hut, he could see everything that went on in his compound.

It was quiet, except for the crack-crack of the dishes and Li's voice above the noise. She was no longer humming but singing rather loudly. Occasionally she wriggled her hips to the rhythm of her own song. Baba unfolded his chair and the clicking sound attracted Grandma's attention. She was about to go into her hut but stopped in the doorway and mumbled some incoherent greetings. Baba, who had opened his book, answered with a nod. Li eyed them both and wondered at their relationship. It was obvious there was no love lost between them. They shared a hatred for each other though this was thinly disguised under a veneer of polite tolerance. Grandma was Baba's stepmother, his own mother having died when he was only six years old. Shrewd and dominating, she had driven three other wives from the household and had ruled father and son with an iron hand. It was rumoured that she had been divorced three times by Kaka, but each time had refused to leave. She had remained inmovable in the family and every mishap was blamed on her presence. Even Baba's fragile constitution had been blamed on her upbringing. Li liked her funny stories but disliked her dirty habits and foul language. Somehow she was glad Grandma wasn't a blood relation.

Li suddenly broke into a popular dirge well known in the dancing arena.

'Li,' her father's voice cut her short.

'Na'am,' she answered politely.

'What was that you were singing?' he asked, flipping the pages of his book.

'A funeral song father,' she answered.

'A what? Did I hear you right?'

'A funeral song,' she repeated.

'No funeral songs in this house,' he ordered. She nodded in agreement and was collecting the dishes ready to enter the cooking hut when her father called again.

'Na'am.'

'Did you hear me speak?'

'Yes, father.'

'Good. I am tired of filthy songs in my compound,' he said and Li let out a sigh. Baba heard and shouted at her. Li turned and stared at him fearlessly. Baba stared back with growing irritation. Suddenly, the irritation turned into anger and he trembled. Li had the power to stir such emotions in him. He thought she was impudent, but it wasn't just this that worried him. It was something else. He hated to admit it even to himself, but there it was, those piercing eyes that stripped him naked and saw through his soul; assessing, judging and condeming him, weighing his strength against his weakness. They were no child's eyes. He had on many occasions promised himself never to show such strong emotion in front of her, but had always broken that promise and ended up feeling like a fool. This was really as a result of an incident that had happened two years before when Li was only eleven years old. Since then her father had always felt extremely uneasy in her presence.

It was on a Friday morning, Baba was getting ready for a prayer meeting twenty miles from the village, when Li rushed into his hut.

'Baba,' she called.

'Yes, Li, what is it?' he asked.

'Baba, do not go to the prayer meeting today. Please do not go!' she pleaded. He stopped fastening his bag and turned towards her.

'What do you mean?' he asked, a little puzzled.

'Something bad is going to happen, really bad,' she said breathlessly.

'Child of the devil,' Baba thought. Then aloud with undisguised irritation, 'What is going to happen?'

'I don't know,' she wavered, embarrassed by his intent gaze, 'but I had a dream last night, a frightening dream,' she began.

He burst out laughing. Li stopped short, cowed.

'Go on, prophetess, what doom did you see?' he said mockingly.

'I was in a strange compound,' she began again, but now unsure of herself, 'in a strange village. There were many people sitting in the dust with their backs to the wall. I walked towards them and peered into their faces, but could not recognise a single person. Their faces were long and sad and nobody spoke to me. Nobody moved or smiled at me. I noticed some had dust in their hair and on their faces. It was strangely quiet. . . as if I was in the graveyard. I panicked and tried to run but tripped over outstretched legs. I screamed and bolted away from the courtyard. Outside, in front of the compound, I had to stop because there was an obstacle in my way. I took a closer look and discovered fresh, brown mounds all over the place, ten, twenty, thirty. . . I screamed and woke up.' Li was trembling at the memory of the dream. Baba was quiet now and listening to her.

'Baba, I have a strange feeling something bad is going to happen. I had this feeling during the dream and I still have it now.' There were tears in her large, round eyes. Baba looked at her for a long time, wondering what kind of child she was. He didn't know how to tackle a child with such a strong inclination towards evil. 'I must discourage her,' he thought. By now Li was thoroughly embarrassed under his silent gaze.

'Yes, what a strange dream for a child your age,' he said finally. 'Look, Li, you are imagining things. This is the work of the devil.'

'Yes, Father,' the poor child replied foolishly.

'Stop thinking about bad things. Your dreams at night are simply what you think about during the day. There is nothing in this dream. Forget it, child.'

He made to put his hand on Li's head, but she dodged. Wiping the tears that had started streaming down her face, she left her father's presence. Somehow she felt cheapened in his eyes. Li had always hung on to her father's words as the ultimate truth but, somehow, what he had said about dreams being reflections of earlier thoughts did not sound right to her. She knew there wasn't a streak of evil in her and she never thought of bad things during the day. If her daydreams were anything to go by, she should be dreaming about paradise. One thing was clear to her, something bad was going to happen, whether or not dreams were figments of the imagination. She had had such dreams before and whenever they were accompanied by a certain weird sensation, which she had come to recognise, something always happened. She kept quiet for the rest of the day, unable to confide in anyone for fear of being ridiculed.

It was late afternoon and the shadows had started to lengthen when a procession of three lorries arrived at the Memorial Hospital. Nobody seemed to have taken much notice of the vehicles, until a bell rang twelve times. It was the death signal of the missionaries. At almost the same time, a woman came running from the direction of the hospital, wailing at the top of her voice. Panic broke loose in the village. People started running in all directions, but mostly towards the wailing woman. Amidst the barking of the dogs, women in a state of confusion, could be heard calling or cursing their children. Everyone was asking everyone else what had happened. The woman was surrounded immediately by a group of people, but she was too shaken and breathless to speak coherently. She simply pointed in the direction of the hospital.

'Accident,' she gasped. 'Terrible, ghastly accident from. . . a. . . neighbouring village. Go and see for yourselves. God. . . what a sight.'

Li ran all the way to the hospital. It seemed the whole village had turned out. There was a lot of pushing and shouting. People whose relatives had gone to the prayer meeting that morning, and others, who had daughters married to men from that village, were frantic with worry. The confusion was largely caused by people trying to rescue their relatives from among the bodies that were strewn on the hospital lawn. The injured groaned and writhed in pain among the dead, some asking for water. A little apart from the crowd, a middle-aged woman sat, covered in red earth, her legs stretched out in front of her. She was stripped to the waist. Both hands were clasped to her breasts. Her eyes were wild and slime ran from the corners of her mouth. She had lost two sons in the disaster and was demented with grief.

The hospital officials had been alerted and were coming in

large numbers, asking people to leave the square. It was getting too hot for the injured people, they argued, and the great commotion was disturbing other patients. They were asked to go to the village square and wait. In another hour or two prayers would be offered for the dead and the injured. Names would be called out and people would learn what they wanted to know. The crowd dispersed reluctantly. The few survivors were surrounded and questions were asked. What had happened?

There had been a sudden storm in the morning and the prayer house, which had been in a state of ruin for years, had collapsed, killing thirty-five people. Many more were still buried under the debris. There were at least a hundred casualties.

The villagers exchanged significant looks. Such a thing had never happened before in the history of the people. And in a prayer house too! The previous worst disaster, the old men recalled had happened in a village on the other side of the river. A flood had swept away two families and nineteen people had drowned.

Li ran all the way home. The weird sensation had left her all of a sudden. She entered their hut and wept. Mama, Awa and their grandfather were still at the hospital. Baba was among the casualties, but no one knew the extent of his injury.

The next day he was discharged from the hospital. Beds were scarce and his case wasn't too serious. His right arm was in a sling and he wore a look of sober reflection. The children gathered in his hut. One by one the villagers flocked in to greet him and to avail themselves of firsthand information. Li watched from a distance. She had refused to enter her father's hut, in spite of Awa's shocked protest.


Both of them recalled the previous incident vividly.

'Go away,' he shouted at her, but inwardly he cursed his emotions.

Li entered their hut sighing too. She didn't see how she could go on living with her parents much longer. Their mother was always rebuking her for what she called her forward and tactless manner. 'One day you will kill me in this house,' she had shouted at Li for some undisclosed crime. Li did not understand their mother at all. She knew things were far from right between her parents and that their mother was very unhappy. Whatever faults the children committed, especially Li and Sule, Baba would punish them and afterwards lash at their mother with words. Only the other day he had said to her, 'A heathen woman can only have heathen children. Why I married you is what I can never understand. There were many believing women in my village, but I had to end up marrying from a heathen village. And even after I have civilised you, you still behave like heathens. Of course, the lion cub takes after its mother.' They always quarrelled at night behind closed doors, but nothing escaped inquisitive Li, especially when the child in question always faced Mama's angry scowl the next morning.

She thought of talking to Awa, but quickly dismissed the idea. Awa had a mortal fear of Baba, a fear which made her humble and submissive beyond reason. Awa would never dream of disobeying their father. She often wondered where Li got the nerve to look their father in the face. Li, for her part, could not help feeling irritated by her senior sister and excluded her from many of her exploits. She had to turn to Sule but there were things he, as a man, had to be excluded from. The two, however, got on well and Kaka was their ally. Kaka. The thought of the old man warmed Li's heart. She loved him very much. There was a strong affinity between her and the ancient one. Li often wished he were her father. She wondered how such a warmhearted man could have a lukewarm son like Baba.

Kaka, too, was fond of her. At five feet four inches, with skin the colour of brown earth, a graceful neck and a slender body, Li reminded the ancient one of his own mother. Li's great-grandma had been the village beauty during her time. It was said she could compete with the village maidens even after she had borne thirteen sons and two daughters. When Li was born, Kaka had taken one look at her and burst into tears. Those bright eyes that peered at him from behind a forest of kinky hair, and the brown-earth skin were those of his dear mother. He had then named her 'Mwapu', the fair one.

Li sat on the wooden bed heavily, wiping her wet hands with the end of her wrapper. She raised her arms and reached out for the clothes-line that hung over the bed. With a gentle pull, she brought down a pile of dirty clothes over her head and onto the bed. She was going to tonight's funeral dance and had to persuade Awa to go with her. If she refused, she would have to extract a promise from her to keep quiet. She selected two of her best wrappers. Not that it mattered in any way. By the time the dance was in full swing, it would be difficult to see who was wearing what.

Awa entered the hut shaking her body like a little dog. Small but plump, with an ebony-black skin, she was beautiful in her own way. Mama used to boast that she was the prettiest baby in the neighbourhood.

'Waiyo!' Awa exclaimed, 'I am dying of cold! Give me your wrapper!'

'Um-um,' Li grumbled, examining the wrapper in question. 'I am wearing it to the dance tonight.' Awa stopped in her tracks and stared at her for a moment.

'You?' she raised her eyebrows, removing her wet scarf and reaching for a wooden comb from the bamboo ceiling at the same time. She ran the comb painfully through her thick kinky hair. 'You?' she repeated.

'Yes. You mean you do not know there will be a dance in honour of Pa Dawi tonight?' Li asked.

'I know, but since when have you started going to dances?' Awa asked sitting heavily beside her on the wooden bed.

'I am thirteen, big sister, and you are eighteen. . .'

'Stop reminding me that I am eighteen, Li. I am aware of that,' Awa shouted.

'Well, it is just that our mother was taken to her husband's house at the age of fourteen.'

'What has that to do with the funeral dance?' Awa asked, amused in spite of herself.

'A lot. You stay at home and die an old woman, but don't put obstacles in my way like borrowing my outdoor wrapper.'

'I see,' Awa laughed. 'Well, I really want to watch the dance to the newly composed song. I've heard the dance steps are complicated, but you know how impossible it is to get out of this place.'

Li smiled openly, revealing a beautiful gap in her upper teeth. She jumped up and demonstrated the new steps.

'If you really want to go, just do as I say and we will get there without trouble.'

Awa nodded, amused. 'The chick telling the hen what to do,' she thought wryly.

'Collect all the dirty dishes and a few dirty clothes,' Li continued. 'Don't change your wrapper. Hide the outdoor wrapper under the dirty clothes. Finally tell Mama where we are going.'

'Where?' Awa asked with a glint in her eyes. She was amused at her little sister's intrigues.

'Where else do you go with all the dirt?' Li asked and they laughed quietly.

'You devil,' Awa sounded worried. 'I will come with you, but we won't stay long and you must behave yourself. Someone close to Father might see us. You know very well what he thinks of cultural dances.' Li gave her a pleased wink.

An hour later, the things carefully washed, they sat on a log under a big baobab tree and watched the new dance.

# Chapter Two

'Oh! How I wish I could try the dance steps,' Li piped, wriggling beside Awa on the bench.

'Uhmm, you will do no such thing. You really are forgetting yourself. Besides, people will laugh at your awkwardness,' Awa said.

'Well, at least I'll be noticed. Someone will probably sing in praise of me in the dancing arena.'

'Ridicule you, you mean. And what happens if Baba learns of it?'

'Haba! Big sister,' Li exclaimed. 'Can't you forget Father for a while?'

'We have to be careful, Li,' Awa cautioned.

'He won't learn of this. If he does we'll have to pay.'

'You'll have to pay, you mean.'

'Both of us. We are here together, remember?' she said mischievously.

'Nobody will see me dancing. I could deny it, you know,' Awa said.

'That would be difficult, big sister. You still would have to say where you were when I was dancing.'

'All right, wise one. You aren't going to dance and Baba will never learn of this either,' Awa said lightly.

Suddenly there was applause from the bystanders. Li's attention was drawn to the centre of the arena. A richly dressed young man was pasting a ten-shilling note on a woman's forehead. Li cheered and clapped with the rest.

'That's Alhaji Bature,' she said, pointing to the man.

'And who is the woman?' Awa asked.

'I don't know,' Li said absent-mindedly. 'That is the part I like best,' still referring to the man's action. 'Someone is sure to paste a shilling on my forehead,' she exclaimed.

'You are worth more than a shilling,' a deep slow voice boomed, startling them both. Li turned her head and looked straight into a pair of bold eyes.

'Besides,' the man continued, 'you really don't have to be

in the centre to be admired.'

He was so confident and sure of himself that Li was spell-bound. Awa hardly looked at him but Li was already summing him up. 'He must be new around here,' she thought. 'The dialect is strangely different, something about the accent.'

She observed also that he was good looking, but poorly dressed. As he drew closer, Li noticed his muscular thighs under a pair of brown shorts, which looked like part of a school uniform. Hanging loosely, and barely covering his hairy chest, was a threadbare shirt which had seen a lot of soap and water. Li looked down at his feet and saw a pair of white canvas shoes with one or two toes peeping from a gap.

She looked up and met the owner's proud eyes evenly. Her heart missed a beat. 'By God, the man is attractive,' she thought. He was tall, several inches taller than Li, and a shade darker. He was healthy-looking, almost robust. 'He must spend all he has on food and forget about clothes,' she thought again with amazement.

Now he was smiling at Li. He had an odd habit of casting side-glances. Li felt nervous. She wondered why he didn't seem to notice Awa at all. She smiled back, convinced she could handle him, given the chance. She was becoming aware of her power over men. Not that she had any experience of them yet —perhaps it was the way they fixed their gaze on her body but avoided her eyes. A neighbour once said that only a lover could look into those large eyes. But she knew the man was different, bold and aggressive. She was the first to avert her eyes.

'You are a stranger here?' Li ventured and almost jumped with pain from a sharp jab on her thigh. It was a warning from her cautious sister to take her time. Li turned to look at her with a puzzled expression and repeated her question.

'Be silent, Li, and stop bothering the man,' Awa said angrily.

'No bother,' the young man smiled broadly, looking at Awa for the first time. His eyes rested on her arms and he observed that she too was beautiful, a beautiful shining ebony black. He studied her face carefully and concluded that she must be the older of the two. Her face carried a weight of respon-sibility that was absent in the younger girl. The man observed also that, although she was much smaller, her body was fully rounded and matured. Nevertheless, she was completely over-shadowed by the other's liveliness. 'Yes,' he thought, 'this part of the village has its share of beautiful girls.' Aloud he said, 'May I sit down?'

'Is this not a public place?' Awa countered with dignity. Li gave her a funny look. She sensed that Awa disliked the man and wondered why. After all, they'd only just met. He sat next to Li, leaving a decent gap between them.

'Why aren't you two dancing?' he asked with a puzzled expression.

'The same reason you are not,' Awa answered his question coldly.

She was playing to the tune of a traditional courtship. A woman was not supposed to show interest in a man on their first meeting. His seriousness would only be determined by how well he took a rebuff and how persistently he pursued his woman. The man turned to Li and found her smiling. Ignoring Awa completely, he kept his head inclined towards Li, waiting for her answer.

'The truth is that we don't know how,' Li replied.

The man was not convinced by her reply. 'You don't know how? It can't be true! Every small child in these parts knows the new steps. Are you strangers here?'

'No,' Li replied.

'Well, where have you been hiding?'

'Under Baba's . . .'

Awa's terrible look interrupted her. 'Enough of that, Li. You've poured enough into the ears of a stranger.'

'All right, big sister,' Li said sullenly and they fell silent. Each was lost in thought. Li was the first to break the silence which was becoming embarrassing.

'You haven't told us where you come from.'

The man looked at her mysteriously and maintained silence, then added, 'Or who I am.'

'Or who you are,' Li replied with amusement.

'I am a young man,' he replied with a ghost of a smile.

'Obviously,' Awa said, surveying him from head to toe. 'We can see that much.' She sounded humorous but for the look on her face. Li and the man burst into laughter. Awa could not contain herself and joined in. The laughter helped to establish a more cordial atmosphere and Awa relaxed a little.

'What are your traditional names?' he asked and Li looked at him with a triumphant smile.

'You tell us your name first.'

'No, yours first,' he insisted.

'Uhmm, he is playing hard to get,' Li commented.

'Who wants to get him anyway?' Awa replied, eyeing his clothes once more. The girls giggled. Awa could be funny without meaning to. Awa stood up and took hold of Li's arm. They'd stayed far too long and their parents would soon miss them, but Li protested. They'd only just come, she argued and, besides, the dance was just beginning to warm up.

'Obey your sister, Li,' the stranger put in. 'She knows best.'

Li got to her feet grudgingly. She was a bit disappointed in the man. She had felt he was on her side. Other girls were much more lucky, she thought, and wished she was in one of those so-called heathen homes.

'May the day break well then, son-of-the-chief,' Li said mockingly.

'May we live to see tomorrow, girls. Greet your people for me,' he added.

'Uhmmm,' Awa grunted, 'see who is sending his greetings to my people.' It was a calculated insult which the man ignored completely.

'And who might we say sent his greetings?' Li asked with a suggestive glint in her eyes.

The man, who was also standing by this time, moved closer to Li and inclined his head towards her. But he addressed himself to Awa. 'I am the son-of-the-chief of London Traku, the famous Habu Adams.'

'And pompous too, you might add,' Li said mischievously.

The piece of information had a comic effect on Awa. She stared at Habu Adams for a minute and roared with laughter. She slapped her thighs and hissed, 'By God, I should have guessed you are from London Traku. Only your type comes from there, a typical villager.'

Habu Adams' face clouded for a second, but only for a second. Li looked open-mouthed at her sister who she thought had been behaving out of character ever since the man walked up to them. Calm and collected, she never behaved like this

even in private. She must dislike Habu Adams very much.
It was Li's turn to urge them to leave.

'Let us go, big sister,' she said.

And as Awa bent to retrieve her shoes from under the log,
the two exchanged a meaningful look over her head. They both
knew then that they would meet again that night.

The next morning Baba called all the children, except the
small ones. He stood, feet apart and arms akimbo, scowling
at a large opening in the fence behind mama's hut. When he
saw that they had all assembled, he turned to face them.

'Who went out last night?' he asked, looking at them one
by one in his usual direct way. Nobody answered him and he
repeated the question twice, his face darkening with anger.
Awa gave Li a warning glance.

'I am talking to all of you. Have you lost your tongues?'

Still no one said anything. They looked at each other
furtively. Above their heads a long oiled whip hung loosely
from the end of a bamboo pole. The silence was becoming
intolerable. Suddenly, Li opened her mouth to speak but was
forestalled by Awa.

'Nobody went out as far as I know,' she said uncertainly.

'Then can you explain the gaping hole, Awa?'

'No, father.'

'A dog could have done that,' Li blundered and regretted
it immediately. Her father might be a shortsighted bigot, but
he was no fool.

'Uhmm, a dog. You really want me to believe a dog made
this neat opening, do you?' He reached for the oiled whip as
he spoke. Sule gave Li a look that seemed to say, 'Keep quiet,
let me handle this.'

Sule had known Li went out the previous night. Frustrated
at the thought that all his friends were at the dance, he himself
had been unable to sleep. He had tossed on his bed for hours,
his heart throbbing in rhythm to the drumbeat. He knew the
dance steps and ached to try them in the dancing arena. He
had thought of stealing out over the fence, but dispelled such
thoughts immediately. The dance wasn't worth the disgrace.

At midnight he had gone behind his mother's hut to smoke

a little to ease the tension. He could not smoke inside his hut because Baba had a disturbing habit of barging in on him— a sort of check on his daily habits. He had thought of school and wished the holidays were over. School was much better. He lit a cigarette and immediately nipped at it, burning his finger in the process. A sudden rustling sound had scared him. He quickly dropped the cigarette and stepped on it. He braced himself for a confrontation with his father, but instead came face to face with Li.

'God in heaven, small one, you scared my insides,' he exclaimed, bending low and searching for the cigarette in the clear moonlight. 'See what you have cost me,' he raised his hand to her nose. 'A costly stick and a burnt finger.'

'Ssh, son-of-my-mother, Father might hear us,' Li whispered, coming closer to him. 'I've been to the dance,' she said excitedly. 'I will tell you all about it in the morning.'

'Uhmm,' Sule grunted. 'To the dance, Li?'

'Say nothing to anybody or . . .' she paused a while, 'I might just be tempted to mention this.' She touched the cigarette.

'You know I won't,' Sule said soberly, 'but I am afraid for you though. You shouldn't have broken the fence.' He moved close and examined the fence. 'You are really empty-headed. You should have climbed over the fence.'

'Allah! That's an idea,' she exclaimed. 'I'll remember that another time.'

'If you survive this time,' Sule said. 'Now wait,' he took hold of her arm as she made to leave. 'What are you going to do about the fence?'

'Mend it of course,' she said easily.

'Before morning?'

She thought for a minute and said, 'I don't know. I guess it'll have to wait until morning.'

'Until he sees it, you mean?'

'I will have to get up at cockcrow.'

'Wake me up and I will help you.'

'Thank you, son-of-my-mother.'

'Don't worry, little sister. Aren't we friends?'

'Plotters,' Li said and they laughed quietly. They both heard a slight cough from the direction of Baba's room and stole away quietly. In the morning Baba had forestalled them, much to their horror. They had overslept.

Awa looked at the oiled whip and shot a glance at Li. She too knew who had gone out last night, although she hadn't known how until now. At midnight, she had got up to look for her blanket and had found Li's bed empty. 'Useless child,' Awa had thought. 'She must have gone after that worthless beggar.'

Now, standing in front of Baba who was angry beyond description, Awa wondered what Li saw in that stranger to risk their father's anger. Good-looking, yes, but what woman needed a man for his face? For that was all he had, a face. In those clothes he looked like a market beggar. Why, the shorts hardly covered his buttocks. And he called himself 'the son-of-the-chief'. Awa stifled a giggle at the train of her thoughts. 'No,' she said to herself. 'The man isn't worth the trouble. Li would be in serious trouble if Baba found out. God knows, the girl has the brain of a chicken. She could have climbed over the fence.' For some strange reason she was glad this had happened. If Li was punished, she thought, she might forget about the stranger. But why did she dislike Habu so much? She tried asking herself that question. Surely it wasn't because he looked poor? What had poverty to do with it? After all, no one in her family could present a better picture.

'Awa,' Baba cut into her thoughts.

'Yes, father.'

'Are you sure you know nothing about the hole?'

'No, father.' She was glad he hadn't asked if she had gone to the dance. She wouldn't have known how to answer that.

'I know Sani slept in his mother's hut, because he was ill,' he began. 'Mari is only six and still afraid of the dark. The twins are only four years old, not to talk of Bata who is still a baby,' he pushed on, looking at them one by one. His eyes landed momentarily on Sani's immediate senior. 'Where were you last night, Becki Hirwa?'

'I was in bed, Baba. You can ask mama.' She said and their father nodded, convinced. Li knew what was coming. Baba wasn't getting any answers, so he had started a calculated process of elimination, bent on finding the truant. Well, she would have to own up, she thought. It was the price she had to pay for the clandestine meeting. She braced herself for the ordeal by taking in a deep breath. Her eyes dilated—half with fear half with expectation—as Baba's eyes settled on her finally.

'What about you, Li? Were you at the dance?'

'I was, Father.' Again Li was forestalled—this time by Sule's deep voice which jolted everybody. Li looked up in surprise. Sule was shielding her. Awa looked from Li to Sule and back, obviously confused.

'I had to go,' Sule was still speaking. 'All my friends were there. I could not sleep.'

There was a charged silence. No one moved or spoke. Finally Baba moved in Sule's direction. He stood and faced his son and they stared at each other. Baba had been taken unawares. He knew that Sule was capable of this sort of thing but, somehow, he had suspected Li this time. He could not say exactly why. Was it the mad glint in her eyes when she had said it could be a dog, or was it the furtive glances? Maybe she was trying to protect Sule, or was it the other way round? Whichever way it was, Baba knew someone was lying some-where along the line. What worried him now was, what was he to do with this man-child? He was a man now and it wasn't just his age, but what he stood for. He could beat Awa easily if she erred, no matter how old she was, but not Sule, his firstborn malechild. And to beat a man for going out to dance at night was outrageous. He decided to give him a chance to apologise. That way both could salvage their pride.

'I am ashamed of you breaking a fence like that,' he said and waited. Silence. He fixed Sule with a hard stare and with his eyes begged him to apologise, but Sule stared back, a new kind of look creeping into his eyes. It was a defiant look as if he was challenging his father to a duel. Baba was suddenly infuriated and said to himself, 'What has come over the children of today? They are not only rebellious but complet-ely immodest. Now what am I to do with Sule?' The others sensed Baba's dilemma and moved closer.

Li no longer looked fidgety. Her eyes grew bold. She was beginning to enjoy the drama. Sule had covered for her, but Li knew very well that Sule's heroism was on his own account. There was no way he could have escaped their father's wrath this day, because Li wasn't one to take any beating alone and Sule was well aware of that.

'I went out, and so did big sister Awa,' she would have blurted out. 'As for big brother Sule, he smoked something awful.'

Nevertheless, Li had her good points. Now that Sule had covered for her first, she was going to do the same. If Baba insisted on beating Sule, she was going to confuse the whole issue by confessing. That way Baba would never know who actually went out, and he wasn't one to punish anyone if in doubt. Li smiled wickedly. It seemed to her that that was one of Baba's few virtues.

Awa was in a different frame of mind. She wasn't concerned about Sule's plight. It served him right, she thought. The wayward children must have gone out together—Sule wasn't the type to stand up for anybody, not even Li. Now he was in real trouble and Awa couldn't help wanting to see his ego deflated. She moved closer and waited for what seemed like an eternity for the drama which never came.

Her father stood with one hand holding the whip loosely, and the other resting on his hip. His shoulders drooped and his eyes looked tired. Presently, Baba dropped the whip and turned to go into his hut. 'What an impotent gesture,' Awa thought.

Li and Sule smiled mischievously at each other. Awa felt like a traitor. 'What an affinity between two people,' she said to herself. 'Why, they should have come as a husband and wife, not as a brother and sister.'

She turned to leave and was arrested by a loud guffaw from behind. Grandma was laughing wildly. She had been watching the scene from the security of her courtyard. 'Foolish man,' she murmured toothlessly. 'He is never tired of playing god with his children.' Her mouth twisted into a funny smile. 'Crack, crack, crack, crack'. The shells of the groundnuts were gradually piling high between her legs.

Kaka walked in slowly, muttering to himself. He stopped abruptly and surveyed the courtyard. The atmosphere was tense. The air, polluted with hostility, assailed him. He watched his son disappear into his hut and observed mama's grim expression as she walked past him. Kaka knew then that there had been another explosion in his absence. He always knew when there was one—people behaved strangely. With a tottering step, he crossed over to his yard.

The twisted smile on Grandma's face confirmed his worst suspicion. 'The witch,' he thought. 'She is never happy until there is trouble in the family. Wicked, barren woman.' In Kaka's opinion, the woman had been the root of all his troubles and of his son's too.

But deep down in his heart, he knew Grandma wasn't the only reason for his son's abnormal behaviour. Other things helped to confuse his sense of moral values. Mainly the quest for modern living coupled with a foreign culture, a thing that was sweeping the whole community like wildfire.

Kaka covered his mouth with the back of his hand and let out a loud yawn. Many things his son did went against his own sense of judgement, but who was he to talk? He was only an old man and nobody listens to old men these days.

In fact his stay in the compound was on condition that he refrained from questioning or interfering with the family's life-style. He stayed but lived a different life, unknown to most members of the family. When he felt sick, he visited Heman, the herbalist, in secret. Of the hospital he had this to say, 'How can a stranger know the diseases of the people? What does he know about the wrath of the gods of my ancestors? Let those that are beginning to go funny in the head swallow white clay for medicine and have their stomachs slit open for a cure.' In the privacy of his room he worshipped his gods. Behind the Hill Station, among the hills, he sacrificed to the gods of his ancestors. Whenever there was a Christian or Muslim festival in the village, he attended both diligently. 'At least there's a man alive who is trying to keep the village clean,' he would say to his friends.

Kaka could have lived peacefully this way, deriving comfort from his private activities, but for what he termed his son's mad obsession with discipline. He could not close his eyes to the constant beatings that took place at the slightest pretext in the name of discipline. He decided to speak to his son in spite of the warning to keep quiet. Children shouldn't be caged, he reasoned, for if the cage got broken by accident or design, they would find the world too big to live in.

Already the cage was too small for most of them. A week ago, Kaka had gone to ask the price of a goat from a neigh-

bour who brewed home made beer, burukutu. He had found
Sule there among friends having a good time. For both their
sakes, Kaka had made a big show of not seeing him there.

Yesterday, too, he had passed by the dancing arena on his
way to visit a sick friend. He had seen his two granddaughters
talking with a tall, young man. Kaka had wondered if that
was the first time they had met. The man had seemed sure
of himself, inclining his head towards Li as he spoke.

'Men are utterly shameless and callous these days,' he had
thought disapprovingly. 'He speaks to a woman even before
he's met her parents. He could be speaking to the daughter
of a leper or a lunatic or, worse still, the daughter of the
accursed.'

He chuckled to himself now. 'This is what they call modern
living.'

His mind came back to the present crisis in the compound.
He wouldn't be surprised if it had something to do with the
girls' presence at the dance yesterday. His son never went out
due to his fragile constitution, but he had a strong nose and
he could smell a rat a mile away.

He sighed and drew up his rickety chair close to Grandma.
'What happened?' he asked in a conspiratorial whisper as he
made to sit down.

'Where?' she asked contemptuously without looking up.

He stared at her bent head for a second and flopped into
the chair. 'In this compound, of course, where else do you
think?' His tone was now one of suppressed anger.

'Nothing happened,' she replied nonchalantly.

'Don't nothing me, woman. You don't wear that face in this
house for nothing,' he shouted at her.

'Which face?' she asked stubbornly.

'Your silly twisted face,' he answered angrily.

'My face,' she said, 'has always been silly in this house. As
for being twisted, your abusive tongue is enough to twist a
virgin's face. Listen, friend, why do you bother to look for
answers to your daily problems on my silly twisted face? You
had better ask your precious son if you want to know what's
happening in your family.' She continued to shell the groundnuts as she spoke.

Kaka was silent for a long time. He cleared his throat and

finally said, 'Thank you for your advice, and now listen to mine, woman. Next time anything happens in my absence, you scrub that dirty face well before I come in, or else I will scrub it for you.' He fell silent and she raised her head for the first time to see if he had finished with her. He seemed to have.

'Ei ei ei,' she cackled. 'I shouldn't be surprised, friend. It sounds all too familiar. It must be in the blood.'

Kaka got up angrily, knocking his chair over. Her mirthless laughter followed him to his hut.

# Chapter Three

It was extraordinarily cold. The dry and dusty harmattan wind blew relentlessly, making it impossible to see beyond a few yards. The village was already alive with activity because it was Tuesday morning, the village market day.

Li had to go to the market early to buy eggs for her father, in spite of the chilly weather. Eggs would be scarce later on in the day because the Hill Station houseboys would buy them in dozens. She rubbed her hands together and adjusted her headscarf over her ears, increasing her pace at the same time. Her bare arms felt as cold as stream water and she clenched her teeth to keep them from chattering. She mustn't seem to shiver. Young people, especially women, were not supposed to feel cold.

The road to the market suddenly seemed to spring into life. Already a few commercial lorries had arrived from some neighbouring villages, bringing goods from the cities. Women, bent almost double under their loads, walked slowly and answered greetings with a wave of the hand. Donkey owners, with mouths muffled under headcoverings, swore and beat their animals. Naked children, their bellies protruding and shining from the early beancake, chased and shouted at each other.

Once inside the market Li took her time and walked slowly, absorbing the early morning scene. The dust increased as stalls were swept. A few people wet the ground to damp down the dust. Li wove her way through the growing din as greetings were exchanged and haggling began. The Kalangu drummers, stationed behind the meatsellers, beat their drums with extra vigour to ward off the cold. A madman, holding a dirty pan, went round the food stalls dancing to the rhythm of the drums and raising more dust in his frenzy. As he moved towards a beancake stall, a fat woman got up angrily and chased him away from her stall. He stopped a few yards from her, and, turning, cursed his mother in vulgar terms. Some of the men stopped what they were doing and burst into laughter. Li avoided the madman. She knew a young woman was an easy target for his abusive tongue.

She walked slowly to the egg stalls and sat on a wooden bench to wait for the traders to unload. A little later, she experienced that feeling of being watched from behind. Slowly she turned her head and met Habu Adams' steady gaze. She became uneasy. Little details about her appearance began to worry her. Her wrapper, she thought, was on the faded side. Her lips were cracked by the severe harmattan wind and her eyes were full of dust. But she smiled shyly and lowered her eyes. Habu approached hesitantly as if he, too, was unsure of himself. He stopped just inches from her and greeted. 'Did you sleep well?'

'Yes and you?'

'Very well, no trouble,' he said 'And your people?'

'They are well except my father.'

'Assha!' he exclaimed, 'How bad?'

'Well, we thank God,' Li said.

'Assha! Can I come to the house?' he asked and Li opened her eyes wide in panic.

'No,' she said.

'Don't worry, I will make no trouble for you,' he said, and she relaxed visibly.

'How is it you are here so early?' she changed the subject.

'I live near by,' he turned round and pointed to a compound a few yards away. 'There.'

'But that is Heman's place—the herbalist,' she was puzzled.

'Yes, he is my father's brother.'

'Your father's brother?' she looked at him in amazement. 'You didn't say you were from this village?'

'I am not, and my father's brother isn't either. He took refuge here about forty years ago, after serious trouble with a kinsman.' Habu explained reluctantly.

'Trouble with a kinsman? What about ?' Li inclined her head towards him, her large eyes full of curiosity.

Habu was silent for a while. He felt a vague need to be cautious about his background. He came round and sat at the edge of the bench. Li moved further away to the other side. She watched as a large fly settled on a small wound on his ankle. Swearing, he slapped at it hard and rubbed his blood smeared fingers in the dust. Li winced and closed her eyes for a minute.

'I am not sure,' he said elusively in answer to her question. 'But I think it was to do with a woman.'

'Ah ha!', Li clapped her hands with glee. 'Was she beautiful?'

'Extremely. She was the village beauty at the time,' he boasted and immediately felt ashamed. 'That was the story I heard,' he added uncertainly. 'It could be true as the woman is still good-looking in her late fifties.'

'And your father's brother, wasn't he married at the time?'

'He was. Two wives and twelve children.'

'What was the story?'

'I don't know,' he said again uncomfortably.

Li smiled mischievously.

'What?' he asked puzzled.

'Oh, nothing,' she said. She was remembering the night of the dance and his eager hands fondling her waist beads. She wondered how much of the uncle was in him. Did such things run in the blood? Aloud she said, 'I had better buy the eggs now. My mother will be waiting for me.'

'Can I see you tomorrow?' he whispered and narrowed his eyes to slits. 'The moon will be full and there'll be singing and dancing in front of the Ward Head's compound.'

Li wanted to add, 'and fondling and playing hide and seek.' Instead, she shook her head. 'I can't come.'

'Your age-group will be there,' he pleaded.

'I know, but. . .'

'Young woman,' an egg seller interrupted her. 'If you are here to buy eggs, you'd better come before they are finished.'

'Good advice,' a second person concurred. 'He,' pointing to Habu, 'is always available, but not the eggs.'

'There was general laughter and Habu got to his feet. The men were enjoying themselves at his expense. He knew he had to leave immediately to avoid further embarrassment, but another attempt to arrange a meeting with Li was necessary. He tried again.

'What about the school grounds?'

'The children-of-my-mother go to school there.'

'What about the woods?' he pursued.

'I don't know,' she said, but on second thoughts she added,

'My sister Awa and some friends are going to the woods on Friday, a week from today.' She excluded herself deliberately.

'Which direction?' he asked.

'I do not know,' she said again.

'The Hill Station?' he coaxed.

'Maybe,' she answered.

He moved closer to her and quickly slipped a ten shilling note between the folds of her wrapper. He had left before she realised what he had done. Li moved and the note fell out to the great amusement of the traders.

'That is a fortune, is it not?' said one of them.

'Today's market is meant for you,' said another.

'But ten shillings, what a big leak that must have made in his pocket, and come to think of the pocket. . .' He guffawed and the rest followed suit.

'That is enough,' an elderly man cut them short. 'Without doubt, you are her father's age-mate. Are you envious that the sun has set for you?' Gradually the laughter died down amidst many protests.

Li bent gratefully and retrieved the fallen note. On getting up, she came face to face with Grandma, who gave her a knowing look. Li cursed the old woman under her breath. 'What could have brought the old witch into the market so early in the morning?' She quickly bought the eggs and left for home.


The next day, Li had to pass the cassava farm to reach the riverside. She had been asked to fetch water in place of Awa who had been sent to the hospital to buy some drugs. Although there was well-water all over the village, Baba would not drink from a well. 'People throw in all sorts of dirt,' he complained. Only a few days before a woman picked up a headscarf out of the well next to his house.

She balanced the water calabash on her shoulder and held it in place with one hand. When asked why she used a calabash or a pot like an elderly woman, she would say, 'weight on my head would eventually shorten my neck. Besides, a flat-bottomed tin would ruin my hairdo!'

She walked briskly humming to herself. A few yards away Li saw the owner of the cassava farm weeding. She drew near, knelt on both knees and greeted him.

'Grandfather, did you sleep well?'

The old man raised his head a little, resting the palm of his hand on his knee, the other hand still held the hoe. On seeing Li, he straightened up slowly with a loud grunt.

'Now, let me see. Who do we have here?' He stared at Li for a long time. 'I can't believe this,' he teased when he recognised her. 'My wife coming to court me right inside my farm?'

Li laughed. The old man was her grandfather's age-mate and bosom friend. He looked much older than Kaka, although he was a few years younger.

'How are you, child?' he went on.

'Well, Grandfather.'

'How is your grandfather?'

'He is as strong as a horse,' she enthused.

'I believe you. I envy the ancient one. You never allow him to grow old. Tell him one of these days I'll challenge him in the dancing arena over you,' he said with mock seriousness.

'You don't have to, Grandfather,' Li coaxed. 'I love you more, you know.'

'Now listen to that!' he laughed. 'By the gods of my ancestors, you have been saying the same thing to him every day of your life.'

'No, Grandfather, listen. You know Kaka is growing old. Nowadays I don't even bother to give him kolanuts or meat to chew.'

'Listen to her,' he beamed, 'and me?'

'Haba! You are young, a little below ninety. Aren't you?' she teased.

'Yes, and I can still chew a kolanut,' he said and Li make a sound of disbelief. 'With a little help from the grinder,' he added and the two burst into laughter. 'How is your father, child?' The old man's tone was serious now.

'He isn't well,' she replied.

'How bad?'

'Bad enough to keep him in his hut, but we thank God.'

'Greet him for me, my child, and tell your grandfather I'll see him tonight. . .in the usual place.'

'Yes, Grandfather.'

'Greet your mother.'

'Yes, Grandfather.'

'Go well, child.'

'Thank you, Grandfather.'

She moved away quickly, her mind engrossed in other things. She was inches away from Faku before she saw her. Faku carried a heavy tin of water and swung her hips from side to side as she walked.

'So, it is you, Li!' she said as she came in level with her friend.

'By God, it is you Faku!' Li exclaimed excitedly. 'It is hard getting to see you, but I was going to look for you on my way home.'

'It is hard getting to see you, not me. You hardly step out of your compound,' Faku replied.

'You know how it is with us at home, but we have to meet somewhere. I have news for you,' she said slapping her friend on the shoulders.

'You have?'

'By God, I have.' Li felt exultant, swearing freely away from home. She had a mental picture of her father's enraged expression could he have heard her.

'What is the news about?' Faku prompted.

'I'll save it for when we meet to talk.'

'Uhmm. From the look in your eyes, it has to be a man.' She looked eagerly at Li to see if her guess was right.

'How do you know?' Li asked, surprised.

'That was what my mother said to me yesterday. "Faku",' she mimicked her mother. ' "Even a blind man can feel the burning in your eyes. Who is he this time?" ' Faku laughed, wiping tears from her face.

'Your mother said that?' Li asked, thinking how close Faku must be to her mother to talk with her about such intimate things. 'You have met someone then?' Li pursued.

'Yes, but we are talking about you, not me.' Faku shifted the weight on her head to one side.

'Let us meet somewhere,' Li said.

'What about tonight, in front of the Ward's Head compound? The moon will be full.'

'I know.'

'Can you come?'

'No.'

'Select the time and place then,' Faku said.

'The woods. Come with us to the woods.'

'When?'

'Next Friday at dawn.'

'I'll ask my mother,' Faku said as she made to pass.

'I can't wait for Friday,' Li said.

'Nor can I. Is he someone I know?'

'I doubt it,' Li shouted over her shoulder. 'He is a stranger.'

'Mine too,' Faku called back as they went their separate ways. 'Is he handsome?' still over her shoulder.

'Like a god,' Li replied and they burst out laughing.

Li walked happily, her feet barely touching the ground. Suddenly, she stopped short, her heart missing a beat. 'Now wait,' she addressed herself. 'Did she say "mine too"? Allah! How many strangers do we have in this small village?' She heard voices and looked back. Some elderly women, Mairama and Hauwa, were a few feet behind her. She gave herself a mental shake and increased her speed. 'I musn't think like that,' she kept telling herself. 'There must be a lot of men out there I haven't met.' All the same, the nagging feeling remained and Faku's excited voice kept coming back, 'mine too, mine too, mine too.'

Li stood in the middle of the courtyard dangling a broom. Sweeping the courtyard was her last chore for the day. She mentally divided the courtyard into four. Standing in the middle, she started sweeping in the direction of the younger children's hut. She figured the largest pile of rubbish came from that direction. Her movement was deft. She could sweep the whole compound with her eyes closed, having been accustomed to such chores since the age of five.

She sang quietly to herself. Life was much more resting now. At least she could tolerate the situation at home better than before. The stolen moments with Habu made up for what she suffered at home. She had Sule to thank for this. Recently Sule had made friends with Habu during drinking sessions. This of course was unknown to Li. All she knew was that Sule had made it possible for the two of them to meet secretly on several occasions. 'Just like Sule,' she thought to herself, 'to like what I like.'

With a smile on her face she turned to survey her work and once more came face to face with Grandma. Li's smile was quickly replaced by a sullen look. She thought that the old woman had a frightening way of stalking people and ought to have been a hunter. She bent down to continue her work.

'Are you not going to greet me, co-mate?' the old woman asked, using the teasing term affectionate grandmothers use for their granddaughters. Li became alert. Grandma was using that voice that says 'I'm after something.'

'Did you sleep well, Grandma?' she greeted without interest.

'I should have, co-mate, if my salt-pot hadn't been empty.' She winked.

Li sensed what was coming next and armed herself with excuses.

'I wish I were still young,' Grandma continued with mock seriousness.

'Come to the point, you witch,' Li thought. Aloud she said, 'What would you have done?'

Grandma was silent for a moment. Li knew she was treading on dangerous ground by prompting her to talk, but curiosity got the better of her.

'I didn't need to do a thing,' she replied. 'I was good to look at. My breasts were the size of backyard pumpkins and my buttocks the envy of the village maidens. The men could not resist me. You know I have been married fourteen times, and each time. . .'

'You have said so, many times before, Grandmother,' Li interrupted.

'Yes I have, but the point is that I met each one of them in the market place.' She let out a shrill, mischievous laugh. Li straightened up and looked at her nervously.

'What do you want, Grandma?' she spat the words.

'Oh nothing, co-mate. Just that my salt-pot is empty and your miserly grandfather will neither part with a penny nor eat a saltless soup.'

'So why do you come to me? Why not my mother?' she asked, knowing well why the old woman chose her.

'Co-mate, I am certain your mother's salt-pot is also empty. Not all of us are lucky enough to earn money in the market place these days. And from what I heard, the young man is rich in spite of his loin cloth.' She laughed again, slapping her thighs.

Scowling, Li dropped her broom and rushed into their hut. Soon she emerged, her fingers tightly closed over something which she thrust into her grandmother's outstretched hands before resuming her work.

The old woman opened her palm and counted the coins with glee. 'Next time co-mate, hide under the cover of darkness or else. . .' her voice trailed as she saw Awa's shopping calabash above the fence. She quickly turned to leave, but not before Awa caught the tail of her sentence. Awa looked curiously at her retreating figure. She disliked and mistrusted the woman and paid little attention to her intrigues, but as she walked past Li, she asked her what the old woman wanted.

'Nothing,' Li replied without looking up. Awa put her shopping calabash into the cooking hut and went into her mother's hut.

# Chapter Four

On Friday at dawn, Awa, Li and Faku headed towards the hills behind the Hill Station in search of firewood. The morning was cold and still dark so that objects could be made out only vaguely. Awa carried a big clay jar of water. Li and Faku followed, their cutlasses balanced on their heads. They walked silently, their footfalls the only audible sound. None of them dared speak under the still darkness. As they approached the Hill Station, they moved instinctively closer to each other. A dog barked nearby and another, further away, responded. They quickened their steps. Li couldn't catch up with the other two and called to them in a hushed whisper.

'Stretch your legs, Li! You aren't a child any more,' Awa answered her angrily. The dog kept drawing nearer until a whistle sounded in the distance and the barking stopped abruptly. Relieved, they slowed their pace.

An hour later, they reached the sacred rock; a big boulder balanced expertly on three smaller ones, leaving a wide, deep cave underneath. The popular belief was that the gods of the village were housed there. No one knew the truth except a few elders who kept sealed lips. However, youngsters were always warned to desist from entering the cave. Li wondered what was really there. She was sure not even wise grandmother knew. As a small child, she had heard all sorts of stories, some of which were incredible. One was about a strong-headed boy who entered the cave, in spite of his grandmother's warning, and was never seen again. But the next morning a slaughtered ram was found at the mouth of the cave.

Grandma, who had told the story, bragged to the children that some day she would enter the cave.

'And get lost or slaughtered?' Li had asked, bewildered.

'Never,' was the throaty reply. 'I understand the language of the gods. I was once a priestess of the goddess of the hills.'

Li smothered a giggle now at the mere thought of Grandma being a priestess of any god. She even doubted the authenticity of the story, considering that grandmother was fond of making up her own stories.

It was clearer now and objects could be identified more easily. They climbed the rocks cautiously, casting fearful glances at the giant boulder that loomed large, dwarfing the smaller ones. Li removed her sandals for a firmer grip on the slippery rocks. Awa adjusted the clay jar. Holding it with both hands, she walked with confident steps. Although Faku was much heavier than the other two, she walked with surprising agility.

Suddenly, Awa stopped dead and motioned to the rest to do so. A little ahead of them a man was sitting very still on a rock, his back to them. A straw hat, was carelessly pushed to the back of his head.

'What is it?' Faku asked fearfully.

Awa put a finger to her lips and pointed in the direction of the man.

'It is nothing, big sister,' Li said loudly, advancing confidently in the direction of the man. 'Haven't you ever seen such a thing before? It is set up by farmers to scare monkeys and birds.'

'Do not believe it, children-of-my-mother. The thing there is much more than a garment and a hat. It has substance.'

Li wondered momentarily if it was Habu playing a trick on them. Only she knew Habu was coming. A woman would not talk to another woman about such a secret arrangement for fear of being ridiculed. If the girls met with any of their suitors during the day, they would pretend the meeting was coincidental or, better still, that the boy had tracked them down in a desperate attempt to see and talk to his woman. She knew Habu would come unfailingly, but not at this unearthly hour. She convinced herself, therefore, that the figure on the rock could not be him. Awa motioned to them to move closer. Knowing well she could not move fast with a jar on her head, she placed it between three rocks.

'Li,' she called softly. 'Use the butt of your cutlass to poke the thing.'

She had hardly finished when the figure sprang upon them. They were petrified for a second, rooted to the ground, but in the next instant the scene was transformed to one of frantic activity. Awa turned to flee and slipped flat on a rock, where she remained motionless, both hands above her head. Li stood with legs wide apart, cutlass raised high in the air. A quick glance showed that Faku had already vanished in the direction of the Hill Station. Not a sound escaped them. The figure took one look at the scene and collapsed in a heap on the rock, helpless with laughter. Two other heads appeared miraculously and joined in.

Awa, who was still lying face down, could not believe her ears at the sound of the laughter. She recognised the voice of Dan Fiama, the village headmaster, popularly known as the HM, and wished she was buried deep under the rock. She raised her head a little and looked at the other two. The figure who had been on the rock was a stranger she had seen briefly in the headmaster's office, but whom she had heard a lot about in the village. The other was Li's soundrel, Habu Adams.

Awa got up slowly, ashamed of herself and angry with the boys. She thought, 'These boys, barely twenty, could play tricks on their mother's sister.' She brushed the front of her wrapper fiercely, trying to regain her composure.

Li laid her cutlass on the rock and glided towards them menacingly. She was slightly embarrassed by the presence of the headmaster. Nevertheless, she made no attempt to hide her rage. Awa watched her sister with keen interest and thought she saw masculine traits in her. Standing in front of them, she challenged them to physical combat, 'Cowards,' she said, 'What were you trying to prove?' No one answered her. They just stared ahead of them, each stifling a laugh. For the second time that morning, Awa felt painfully humiliated. She turned and sat down on the nearest rock. Habu followed her lead. The stranger, having moved several places away from them, was whistling tunelessly. The headmaster busied himself collecting pieces of rock.

Li, still angry, accosted Habu, saying, 'They tell me strangers are no good. I think they are right. Who is the other stranger?'

'He is no stranger, Li,' Habu explained. 'His name is Garba, and he tells me that your runaway friend knows him better than I do.'

Li sighed, relieved. 'So that's Faku's mysterious stranger.' She turned her head and looked at Garba closely.

'What in God's name, are we waiting for?' Awa's voice startled them all. 'Can't one of you run after Faku? She must have reached her mother's hut by now.'

They all burst into fresh laughter. The tension that had began to build up fizzled out almost immediately. Garba turned on his heel and sped down the hill.

The headmaster tried to ease the situation further by saying, 'Li, for one alarming moment, I feared you were going to hack Garba to pieces.'

'By the gods of my ancestors, I nearly did,' she said without conviction. Although the joke had been a costly one, it was also funny. She could not confess to them that as she stood there with the cutlass raised high above her head, her shadow, as our people would say, had fled, leaving her empty trunk. In another minute, she could have dropped down with sheer fright.

'You are brave, a he-woman,' the headmaster piped up, eager to make amends.

'More than you think, HM,' she said sarcastically.

Habu looked at her with a curious expression. 'She looked already gone to me,' Li met his eyes evenly and a look of understanding passed between them.

Faku and Garba soon rejoined the group. Faku, covered in scratches, her wrapper in shreds, looked distraught. Breathlessly she related how a branch had caught her wrapper from behind and believing that the apparition had caught up with her at last, she had fled through the bushes, scratching herself badly and only stopped on reaching the Hill Station.

They laughed at her. Still dazed and shaken, she sat on the nearest rock and looked at their faces one by one, her eyes searching for an explanation.

'By God, I didn't know you were such a good runner,' Garba teased.

'By God, I didn't know you were such an empty coward,' she replied.

Now Awa turned to them and demanded to know what they were doing at that time of the day.

'The same thing you are doing,' Garba replied. It suddenly occurred to Awa that Li must have informed Habu about the wood fetching. She eyed Li but found her expression blank.

'Let us go,' Habu urged them on and led the way. They walked in single file, the men in front.

Li's feet began to hurt. Just as she was about to protest about the distance, Habu stopped and lowered himself on to a fallen tree trunk. The others followed, each looking for a place to sit while surveying the scene.

Three huge trees had been felled recently, leaving the stumps naked under the morning's cool breeze. The trunks were neatly chopped into pieces and piled high. Large single branches lay scatterd all over the place. It looked as if a dozen men had been at work for a week. No one spoke for a long time.

Finally Li said, 'Habu how long did it take you three to cut all these?' she gestured towards the scene.

'Five days,' he answered promptly, his voice swollen with manly pride.

The girls exchanged surprised looks, while the young men smiled above their heads feeling proud of their achievement. They knew without being told how deep an impression they had made.

'Five sweaty days,' Garba harped on. 'It is enough bride-price.'

They all laughed. None of the girls suspected that the work had been done by two people only. For five days Garba had lain under the shade of a tree, smoking, while the two younger men worked their fingers sore. A look at the palms of their hands would have been enough evidence.

Awa, still puzzled, turned to face the men who were already relaxing under the shade of a huge tree.

'You knew we were coming to the woods today,' she stated as a matter of fact.

'Yes,' Garba agreed.

'But how?' Awa pursued.

'Easy, women are always going to the woods,' Garba replied.

'No,' Awa said. 'Meeting you at dawn has unsettled me and now this.' She gestured towards the scene as Li had done earlier. 'There is something going on which I do not know about,' she said, looking at them suspiciously.

Habu stole a glance at Li and Awa caught the look. 'Ah ha!' she turned and faced Habu. 'Li told you, did she not?'

After a moment's hesitation Habu grunted in the affirmative.

'Haba!' Awa clapped her hands and shook her head vigorously. 'No wonder she behaved like a man and did not run when he sprang on us! And she knows how to pretend too, standing straight with both arms above her head like a god.'

'No, big sister,' Li protested. 'This is not true. I mentioned to Habu we were coming to the woods today, but how was I to know he would come out at dawn to act the ghost?' The rest laughed but the two sisters remained serious.

'I do not believe you, Li,' Awa went on angrily. 'The meeting was arranged. I should have known you children were up to something mischievous.'

'Girls,' Habu cut in rather too sharply. He hated to be referred to as a child. 'The sun is getting higher,' he announced importantly, 'and the shadows are lengthening. Trim the branches. The rest is a woman's job.'

The girls set to work quietly, while the men watched the rhythmic movements of their bodies, and made small talk about them.

When they finished the girls went and sat with the young men. Although the day was still young, the air was already hot. Everybody was sweating and feeling uncomfortable. The moment all of them had been waiting for had come. but the moment found them acutely self-conscious. Li's attention was drawn to Garba, who sat apart from the group, smoking cigarette after cigarette. He did not seem to notice that Faku had her eyes rigidly fixed on him. Next, Li watched the headmaster as he made several futile attempts to catch Awa's attention and finally gave up, because Awa was deliberately busy making a neat pile of stones in front of her. As for Habu, he was gazing blindly into space, perhaps dreaming of the future.

Once more Li's mind returned to the stranger, Garba. Who was he? She had heard talk concerning him at home and in the village, most of it unfavourable. Somehow she had never associated him with Faku's stranger, because no one had referred to him as a stranger. Li tried to recall everything she had heard about him at home.

One day Awa had come back from school full of excitement. 'Aha! We had a stranger in the school today!'

'So?' Sule raised his eyebrows. 'What's so different about

him or her?'

'Reckless,' was the sharp reply. 'He came roaring in on a motor bike, disturbing the entire school. I thought HM would be furious, but he came out laughing and . . .'

'Clapped the stranger on the back,' Sule finished for her.

'So he did,' Awa exclaimed. 'It's as if you were there.'

'That was no stranger,' Sule explained. 'That was Garba, the son of the soil.'

'But he smoked a lot and swore a lot, Sule,' Awa protested. No one bothered to remind her that some of the villagers did a lot more smoking and swearing than the stranger.

'And,' Li added, 'few people have machines in this village and you know them.'

'Yes, he was brought up in the city but he was born here,' Sule insisted.

'Who are his parents?' Awa asked.

'I do not know, but I told you he is the son of the soil.'

'Indeed, the son of the soil without parents. Who was it told you?'

'He did,' was the sullen reply.

'You know him then?' Li put in. 'Where did you meet him?'

'It does not concern you,' he replied sharply. 'You be careful!'

'Son-of-my-mother, it is you who should be careful,' Awa cautioned. 'He looks bad company for you.'

A week later, on her way to the market, Li had overheard a conversation between two neighbours, Mairama and Hauwa. 'Have you heard?' Mairama asked. 'Pokta's son is in the village.'

'May God have mercy on Pokta's soul. May he forgive him and accept him in paradise,' Hauwa prayed.

'Yes, the poor man needs our prayers. The things he did in his lifetime!' Mairama said smugly.

'Which woman's son is in the village?'

'The prostitute's. The bastard son of the prostitute who lives in the city,' she replied with contempt.

'La! What does he want in the village after so many years? Don't we have enough troubles?' Hauwa cried.

'Maybe to share in the legacy,' Mairama said sarcastically.

'Share in the debts, you mean. We all know the man left

nothing but debts.'

'Who knows the truth in this village?' Mairama said. 'All the same, whatever brings him here, he goes about it strangely. For how does a man go about settling his dead father's affairs? By pouring his money into the beer pot or the game of chance?'

'He takes after his father then?'

'Up to his fingertips.'

'You have to be careful of your female children.'

'You too, take care of your male children. It is contagious.'

Li looked at Garba and tried to guess his age. It was hard to tell. Although he was obviously older than any of them, he had a deceptive figure, stocky and athletic. She guessed he was in his mid-twenties. Her curiosity about him prompted her to break the awkward silence that had settled upon the group.

'Garba, tell us about the city.' Her voice surprised every-body, except Garba who showed no sign of having heard it. He puffed away at his cigarette nonchalantly, his expression blank. He looked far away past everybody as if he was miles away from them.

Finally he said, 'What do you want to know about the city?'

'Anything you can tell us,' Habu replied.

Garba at once plunged into a tireless account of the pleasures of the city. The availability of free women, easy money and idle living. The rest listened without interruption, each engrossed in different thoughts. Some, like Li, were asses-sing his character and wondering what kind of life he led in the city. He talked endlessly, often punctuating his one-sided conversation with a boisterous laugh at his own vulgar joke. Li observed that he was attractive in a coarse way. He would have been good-looking but for his large square nose and wide weak mouth. He had a deep-throated laugh that came in gasps.

It was when he touched on the subject of marriage that the rest became really interested.

'Getting married is not expensive in the city, brothers,' he announced.

'True? I thought it was,' Habu rejoined.

'A girl could live with you of her own free will. Sometimes

you do not have to pay anything,' Garba continued.

'But surely you have to work on her father's farm?' Dan Fiama observed. Garba bellowed with laughter.

'There are no farms in the city, brother. Besides you never get to know a girl's relatives.'

'That is not marriage!' Awa exploded with indignation. 'That's prostitution!'

'You call it what you like, sister, but the point is that one can acquire many wives without slaving for them,' Garba said.

Fiama tried to grasp the point. 'So each woman looks after herself and her children, while the man keeps a common barn?'

'Not exactly,' Garba said with impatience. 'In the city you do not have to live together in the same house. I have a friend who keeps four women in four different areas of the city. None of them knows the others exists and they all slave for him!'

Habu grimaced. Fiama wrinkled his nose in disgust. Garba looked at them sadly and shook his head. 'You do not understand, brothers,' he went on. 'It is much easier that way.'

'It is no way to live,' Fiama argued. 'It kills manhood. How can a woman slave for you?'

'How can he love all of them?' Habu asked. Once more Garba roared with laughter.

'Haba Habu,' he exclaimed. 'Book learning has ruined you. It is a good thing my old woman never sent me to school. What is this love you talk about, friend? Can a man possess a lot?' he asked with sarcasm. No one answered him. 'Come brothers, listen to me.' He drew closer to them, excluding the women. 'I did not live in the city for nothing. I know a bit about the world, more than our fathers who were born and brought up in this small village. There are a lot of things about the city I cannot talk about, simply because such things have no place in the village. But you are young and will soon go out into the world. Only then would you learn from time and experience. Right now you do not believe me, but it does not matter. Some day you will find out I was telling the truth.'

They listened with rapt attention to the city wisdom. Suddenly the headmaster felt ignorant. What did he know about love, that much talked-about word in the village? True, he had been married. His thirteen-year-old bride, who had died in childbirth a few years ago, had been his father's choice. The headmaster had cared a lot for the fragile girl. He had looked after her well when she was ill, thus earning his good reputation as the most loving husband in the village. Yet, whatever he had felt at the time, love or compassion for the child-bride, hadn't prevented him from taking his pleasures elsewhere. If she was too ill to please him, what was he, an adult male, to do? But as for marrying more than one wife, the idea had never occurred to him. He didn't consider himself a suitable candidate for polygamy. He looked furtively at the three girls, his eyes lingering on Li. He shook his head sadly. 'Two such women could render a man impotent.'

The young headmaster wasn't alone in his thoughts. Awa too disliked the idea of polygamy. In her opinion, the children of different mothers disliked and distrusted each other. Also the co-wives were always vying jealously for the husband's favour, thus creating a tense atmosphere in the home.

Faku, however, thought quite differently. What was this love the rest were cracking their heads about? When a man cared for his family, fed and clothed them properly, what was it if it wasn't love? She would like to be Garba's only wife. What woman wouldn't? But if the man could afford to feed a dozen other wives, who was she to object? For her, polygamy wasn't the point at all. The point was that once she married, living alone with her mother was over. They would no longer have to work their fingers sore to feed themselves or mend the leaking roof, because someone else would be responsible. She did not seem to have taken in Garba's gibe about women slaving for men. All she thought of was that Garba was obviously wealthy and as wise as a tortoise. As for her friend Li and her sister, she would give them the benefit of her advice later.

Li, on the other hand, was worried about Faku. She wished Faku would have nothing to do with this man with the shady background. Li knew that Faku had suffered all her life, ever since she was six, when her father had died. Three years later, her two brothers drowned in a flood and she was left alone with her mother. On top of all these tragedies, her mother was branded a witch by the villagers. Perhaps, Li reasoned, Faku was eager to prove to the villagers that she could get married in spite of what they thought of her family.

Again Li's mind went back to the question of Garba's age. 'When did you leave the village for the city?' she ventured.

'Twenty years ago,' was the answer. 'I was twelve then.'

Li let out a gasp. The man was much older than she thought, her mother's age-mate. 'Perhaps,' she said to herself, 'this is what Faku really wants, and as our people would say, "The body grows fat on what the heart desires" so may it be with her.'

It was mid-afternoon, time to go home. They would come again the next day. The girls carried as much wood as they could and set out silently. The men followed at a respectful distance, deep in conversation.

# Chapter Five

Li stumbled out of the dark room into the cool morning air. The breeze caressed her face as she stretched and yawned loudly, causing a stir among the chickens behind her mother's hut. She stumbled drowsily towards the water pot and felt for the small watergourd. She had risen at the first cockcrow and it was still dark. Filling the small gourd with water, she carried it behind their hut to wash.

Minutes later, she emerged, cool and refreshed, and nearly collided with Awa who was also going behind the hut. 'Li, where is the waterpot?' Awa whispered as they passed each other. 'I am going to the stream.'

'On top of the hearth,' Li replied. 'Return well.'

Li collected the cooking utensils and began to clean them. This early morning, she felt the whole world was at her feet. Today was the end-of-year festival and the village would be in a festive mood from dawn to dusk. For a week in every household in the village the talk had been of the big annual dance. It had always been a joyous occasion for the healthy, the strong, the men and women of hot blood. No one would remain at home except the pregnant women, the infants, the infirm and the eccentric. Li knew her household fell into the last category and this day would have passed like any other day, in painful longing. But fate has its own way of dealing with things. Baba was away from the village and would not return for the next three days.

Li smiled a triumphant smile. The previous day she had been unable to look sad as Baba announced their uncle's grave illness. Inwardly, she had blessed her uncle who she thought couldn't have chosen a better time to fall ill.

She closed her eyes and imagined herself dancing tonight under the watchful eyes of the full moon. Clutching her wrapper tightly over her bosom, she tried the dance steps unsteadily.

An hour later, she took a broom and started sweeping. There was a flurry of activity outside, and she peeped between the stalk fence. Grandma was clearing a space, cursing loudly, in which to burn the dung of goats and sheep for potent ash. A few feet away, a group of early risers was forming rapidly. Mairama was the first to come, closely followed by Manu, the hunchback. As they were talking, Hauwa and Audu joined the group.

'Did you sleep well, neighbours?' some voices greeted.

'Well, except for the usual problems,' someone coughed exaggeratedly. 'The woman of my house isn't getting any better and my grandson ails.'

'Uhmm, son-of-my-mother,' Mairama said, 'talking of ill-nesses. I am just a walking illness. I ache all over my body. I haven't slept for days.'

'Days, you say?' Manu joined in. 'I have not slept for weeks.'

'Yours is nothing compared to mine,' Audu put in import-antly. 'I have not slept for MONTHS!'

'Don't tell me that, Audu,' Manu said. 'People with sons in the big city have no problems.'

'Don't talk to me about my son in the city! The city may be big but not my son. Like a woman, he cooks for the big men in the city.'

'Cooks?' Manu laughed affectedly, slapping his thighs.

'Yes, cooks, son-of-my-mother. What other dirty jobs he does for them I do not know. All I know is that every other year he comes home hungry-looking and loaded with problems. One would have thought he would have the sense to feed on what he cooks. For me his homecoming has turned into a nightmare. Next time he comes it will be to visit my grave.'

'Assha, Audu, May the gods forbid it. It can't be that bad,' Hauwa comforted him.

'Worse than you think, my clanspeople. It is what breaks my sleep and adds years to my years. To think my son has turned into a woman! Look at me, always coughing, and their mother never out of bed. Is there another man alive with so many problems?' He looked at them imploringly. 'What have I done to deserve all this? Look at his age-mate, Fiama, a good mallam and a good farmer. What a blessing for the village that he is marrying the daughter of the land!'

'So you have heard?' Manu asked, surprised and dis-appointed. He had imagined the ancient one had divulged the secret to no one but himself.

'It is no secret, son-of-my-mother. Even the deaf can see the blind hear. In this village whatever remains secret has not yet happened. Moreover,' boasted Audu, 'There are no secrets between me and the ancient one.'

'Uhmm,' Mairama grunted, 'maybe there are. That family runs deep. No one can claim to know anything about them.'

'Do I understand you, woman?' Audu turned to her, puzzled. 'I thought you were friends with the ancient one, yet you sound unhappy at the happy news.'

'I am unhappy,' she said slowly. 'I cannot lie to you. The gods will not forgive me. Fiama, the son of my friend, is a good boy. I wish him well, but I wish he would not marry into that family . . .' Her voice trailed off in the direction of the old woman who was still grumbling and casting angry looks at them.

'I know,' Audu smiled. 'It is your daughter, Amina. You have always matched her with him, have you not, daughter-of-my-mother?'

There was an impish twinkle in his eyes. Manu burst into self-conscious laughter, slapping his thighs once more.

Mairama turned on him angrily. 'That's enough, by God! You don't mean he is too good for my child?' She scowled at him so hard that the hunchback shrank visibly. 'No, no, no,' he squirmed. 'I mean nothing like that, just that . . . just that . . . nhe, nhe . . .' Mairama turned her back on him with a gesture of dismissal. To her, as to many other villagers, Manu was a symbol of human failure.

Turning to Audu, she said, 'Can you blame me, son-of-my-mother? If other people's daughters can get husbands, why not Mairama's daughter? And it isn't as if Fiama wasn't interested. Up till now he always kneels on the ground to greet me.' No one dared tell her that Fiama did that to everybody as a mark of his good breeding.

'Be patient, Mairama. There must be other Fiamas in this village.'

'No, there are not. If there are, find one fast, brother. Like your son, the city is changing my daughter. The last time she came, there was no womanhood left in her. She slept until the smallest child was up and the laziest animal had gone to the fields for grazing.'

'Do not worry yourself,' Hauwa consoled. 'Some day she will change.'

'Yes, some day,' she said with sarcasm, 'when all the good boys are married. HM is every woman's dream of a son-in-law.'

'I always say that some women's wombs are blessed and others cursed,' Audu said tactlessly.

Mairama turned on him angrily. 'Do not believe a word of that, my people. It is not the woman's womb but the man's seed. By God, Awa's mother has luck.'

'It is more than luck. It is good training,' said Audu.

'Good training? Eh- eh- eh- ' Mairama laughed maliciously. 'By whom? Can you say the younger sister has good training? Barely fifteen, and always behind barns and bushes with a man! Badly trained, I would say.'

The group was silent for a while, then suddenly they started asking each other questions.

'Whose son is always seen with the younger sister?'

'Heman's nephew, they say.'

'Gods of my ancestors! Isn't that boy full of himself? He walks with his head held high and his cloth barely covering his buttocks. "A naked prostitute" as our people would say.' There was general laughter at this.

'He is better off in his ancestors' dress, a loin cloth.'' More laughter.

'But Heman's nephew, uhmm! Truly that family would give their daughter to the son of a leper.'

'No, it is not the father's fault,' Manu defended vehemently. 'Baba would not have the heathen in his family, but the girl and her grandfather would have no other.'

'I always say the ancient one is deep.'

'Well, there is a better side to it,' Audu joked. 'With those faces and heights, the village should be blessed with stream gods and mountain giants.'

'And when is the happy occasion?' Hauwa asked.

'Just before the rains,' Manu confided. 'Five moons from now, the oldest will be taken to her husband's house, two moons after, the younger one.'

'It is a bad time to give away one's daughters, just when the farm work is at hand,' Mairama commented.

'The man has no choice,' Manu explained. 'The younger of the two daughters is running loose.'

'And our other daughter?' Mairama pointed with her chin in the direction of Faku's compound.

'She has nothing to lose,' Manu went on. 'She comes from bad seed, a cursed family. And if what I hear is true, the city man is no good either. He is rootless.'

'Eh- eh- eh-,' Mairama let out a mischievous laugh. 'My ancestors,' she called, 'See who is talking about bad seed and rootlessness! Surely the world is a funny place.'

Manu fidgeted uneasily and Audu coughed for attention.

'Yes, my clanspeople,' he began with an air of importance. 'Seeds and roots are not important. What is important is what man makes of himself in this life. His ability to succeed in the game of life.'

He looked at them thoughtfully. 'We always ask, "Whose son is he?" or "Whose daughter is she?" We never ask, "Who is he?" Can a man choose his parents? No. Can he help coming from a particular family or clan? No. But my clanspeople, a man can help being who he is.'

He nodded again thoughtfully, savouring his own wisdom. 'May we see another day,' he added abruptly and walked away.

The group broke up. Manu and Mairama walked towards the compound. As they approached the main gate, Li slipped behind her mother's hut. It was a promising morning, she reminded herself. She mustn't jeopardise it by seeking luckless people, a notorious gossip and an imp . . .

Half an hour later, Grandma was deep in conversation with Mairama. Li could see the old woman gesticulating wildly. Gradually her shrill voice rose above Mairama's quiet one. Li could not hear the words at first so she stopped what she was doing and listened.

'Bastard son of a witch!' Grandma was saying. 'Cursed by your people and disowned by your father! She-man with the head of a man and the finish of a woman! If indeed you are a man show yourself in the dancing arena today. Clear yourself of the insults and stop sending your goat to eat my cornflour. Can't you see, son of the witch, that real men do no such mean thing? I warn you,' she gestured to no one in particular, 'next time the goat dips its smelly nose in my flour,

I'll castrate it, just like its master!'

Li winced and glanced towards the direction of her grandfather's hut. Manu was still in there, apparently listening to the tirade and unable to venture out. By now small children had surrounded the old woman, their ears drinking in the torrent of abuse. Each time she said something really vulgar, they laughed and clapped. Several younger women could be seen peeping between the stalk fences.

The men went about their business nervously, not daring to walk in the old woman's direction. They knew very well that in this ugly mood, she could extend her insults to the menfolk in general. Only the other day, she had sat on top of her barn and facing the ward had addressed the menfolk.

'Men of this village,' she had shouted. 'Listen to my words. I was married fourteen times in the eastern part of this land. I left for this part because I could find no lion among them. The village was filled with red monkeys, black monkeys, jungle pigs, wild cats, toothless dogs and lame cocks. Did I know, gods of my fathers, that I was coming to meet a worse pack? This village is full of lizards, snakes, worms and by the gods of my ancestors, cold slippery fish.' She bellowed with laughter. 'And the women? A pack of domestic donkeys with no shame. When they are not under the whip of their wizard husbands, they are busy plotting witchcraft.'

That day was bad, but today was worse. This time without mentioning names, she had made it clear to her listeners whom she was abusing. She took a broom and began to clear a space where she would soon spread the ears of her corn to dry. Manu, thinking she had gone into her hut, sneaked out of grandfather's hut and made for his hut. Too late he saw her. As he passed her, the old woman bellowed with laughter.

Manu had always been a miserly bachelor, until a serious illness compelled him to marry. Li would always remember the marriage ceremony that turned out to be a rare event indeed. A popular musician was invited to play and people turned out in dozens to see the notorious woman-hater turned woman-lover. The speech Manu made was equally memorable. The gist of it was that after years of loneliness, he had discovered that 'everyone needs someone who cares in order to survive.' However, Manu was careful to warn the bride and the community that unlike privileged men he had 'absolutely nothing to offer to a woman, but hard work'. He hoped the woman would be satisfied. On his part, he explained, he was satisfied in the knowledge that when he died there would be someone to mourn and bury him.

That was good enough for the crowd. He was applauded, congratulated and patted on the back for his seeming honesty and modesty. There wasn't another man in the whole village as sincere as the hunchback. No one knew or even guessed the implication of that speech. No one knew how little he had to give.

A year later, the bride packed her pots neatly. She wished to leave. Men and women elders were called in to question her, but she would not answer. They tested, pestered and finally threatened her until at last she screamed out: 'No, I cannot stay, age-mates of my father, no:

My blood is hot, but my flesh is famished,
I fear I will burn to ashes.
The rains have come, the field is prepared,
But my field remains untilled.
Do not ask me to stay, my clanspeople.
Who can stand the sneaking whispers of the wicked
    market women?
Who can avoid the mocking looks of the age-group?
Who would rebuke the innocent children when they
    call me barren?
Who, indeed, can stop the wagging tongues of my
    enemies in the dancing arena?
Age-mates of my father,
Have you an answer to my plight?'

The elders, with downcast eyes, had started leaving one by one even before she had finished. They regretted asking deep questions. Without meaning to, they had stripped their clansman naked for all eyes to feast on. They knew what had transpired that day would spread like wildfire on harmattan grass. The next thing would be Manu's name in the village arena. He would be ridiculed in songs and would carry the shame of it to the grave. What fate had compelled them to probe? As the Hausas say, 'The chicken is better left in its

54

feathers'. Indeed, that way you never know how thin it is.

Li shook her head sadly at the memory. She had not under-stood these things then, but as she grew older, a lot of secrets unfolded themselves before her. 'My ancestors,' she said to herself. 'How can it be that the hunchback is also a man like Habu and my grandfather?'

Mechanically she began washing pots and calabashes, her mind divorced from her fingers. She was dreaming of a paradise called the 'city'. A place where she would have an easy life, free from slimy calabashes and evil-smelling goats. She looked down at her coarse hands and feet. One of these days she would be a different woman, with painted nails and silky shining hair.

She was going to be a successful Grade I teacher and Habu a famous medical doctor, like the whitemen in the village mission hospital. The image of a big European house full of houseboys and maids rose before her. Li smiled to herself. The bushy stream, the thorny hillside and the dusty market would soon be forgotten, in the past.

Ever since the chance meeting with Habu in the dancing arena, Li had lived in a dream world. She swung her hips as she walked, her feet barely touching the ground. Her face had that peculiar glow that is derived only from an inner happiness.

Baba watched her with growing anxiety as she got out of his control. The only restraint came from her grandfather, who would say gently, 'You mustn't do that my mother. That will be the death of me.' Or, 'I cannot prevent you from doing that, mother, but prepare my shroud first. I may not live to see the end of it.' Li would usually give way with a grudging 'That ancient one will cheat me out of this life.'

# Chapter Six

Four years later, Li, a young woman of nineteen, sat still on a mat, her legs crossed in a meditative position. Resting her chin on the palm of her right hand, she stared blankly into space. She sat like that for a long time. Finally, she shook her head sadly. Drawing a calabash of groundnuts in front of her, she started shelling them.

As her fingers worked, her mind went back over the last four years when her life and her hopes had been different from what they were now. It was strange, she thought, that so much could occur in so short a time. Events had begun to happen fast after the annual dance. That was the night Baba was away visiting with a sick brother. That day was to mark an important turning point in Li's life.

As the drums throbbed and the dancers swung their hips with abandon, Awa, Li and Faku talked loudly in an attempt to be heard above the din. Excitedly, Faku announced Garba's intention to marry her immediately and settle in the city. Garba was 'tired of the village' and yearned to 'go back to civilisation.' Faku had caught the city fever too and could not wait to leave the village. She expressed great pity for the two sisters whom she believed would never be privileged to see the city lights. Turning to Awa, she had said, 'Do you really intend to live in the village all your life?'

Awa had replied, 'Yes, daughter-of-my-mother, we need not go to the city. The city will come to us. The government will soon take over all schools and hospitals. That means rapid development. A secondary school will be attached to the primary school and HM will be the first principal. The last time the Primary School Inspector came, he as good as told him so. The HM promised me an important position in the school. I will be head of the Adult Education Classes for older women.'

As she spoke, new ideas kept flooding her mind and she expanded on them with a depth of feeling strange even to herself. 'I have always wanted to do something big in the village.

This is the chance I have been waiting for!'

Big words, noble intentions. Awa's eyes glowed and her teeth flashed as she wriggled her hips in rhythm to the drums. She was intoxicated by the drums, the full moon and the freedom of the night.

Li too, talked as she never talked before. For the first time, she voiced her plans carefully while others listened with rapt attention. Once more the image of the city rose before her as she spoke: the qualified doctor, the Grade I teacher, the big European house full of servants, the smooth body, the long silky hair. . . There was no end to the luxuries the city could offer. The future, was in their hands. The world was full of wonderful and exciting things. And were they not young and eager and ready to enjoy life to the fullest?

Li shook her head at the memory of the night. 'The gods never missed a word we said that day. We made our plans—they took over.'

Now, four years later, here she was, still in the village, still waiting for Habu, who had become a salesman instead of a doctor. Habu's family had paid the bride-price soon after the dance festival, but Habu had to get a job first in the city. Having found the job he had written to say, 'As a salesman, I am always travelling. You will be alone in the city, so wait at home until I send for you.'

She was still waiting. As the years rolled by, she grew taller, gained weight and lost that gawky look. She was said to be the most beautiful young woman in the village. After two years had passed and Habu had failed to come for her, fresh suitors began to flock in. One of them was the famous Alhaji Bature.

Whenever she passed by men, they would shake their heads and say, 'What man in his senses would leave a woman like this behind? If he isn't capable, there are capable men around. Look at Alhaji Bature, son of the soil, rich and prosperous and ready to marry her, yet she will have nothing to do with him. Truly our ancestors were right when they say, "where there is a rope, there is no load and where there is a load there is no rope." '

At first she got the sympathy of the villagers, but as the years passed they began to ridicule her, for waiting for a man who was no longer interested in her. 'That husband of your daughter,' they would say to her mother 'is no good. He is as slippery as a fish. A good bait for foolish girls.'

Li continued to wait patiently despite the many tricks employed by Alhaji and the others. But with each passing day, her hopes waned and her hard protective shell began to crack a little at a time. She wished she could confide in someone close to her, but there was no such person. Faku had long gone to the city and was reported to have given birth to a male child. Awa too was not left behind. Two years ago she had twin sons, Hassan and Husaini, and was now expecting another baby.

'Everybody is having children these days,' Li reflected sadly, looking up in time to see her sister Awa walking slowly into their father's hut. She had been home for weeks now to look after Baba whose health had taken a turn for the worse. A few weeks ago, he had collapsed in front of his hut and had become partially paralysed.

Li did not visit his hut. The few times she had been there, Baba had simply stared at her. At first she could not read the meaning of his looks, but gradually she realised that he would rather not have her around. It was then Awa was sent for.

It was incredible, Li thought, that Baba's illness had wrought so much chaos in the family. When he was still active it seemed he brought nothing but unhappiness, yet when he became paralysed the compound went beserk.

'I have seen two hundred seasons,' Kaka lamented the other day. 'I haven't the strength to run after feather-footed children.'

'Li!' the ancient one's voice interrupted her reverie. She looked up quickly in time to see Bala, a one-year-old baby, crawling happily towards the glowing hearth. She had almost forgotten her charge. Bala represented another unlooked-for development that had done much to divide the family and the pattern of their lives.

Bala was Sule's first child by the daughter of the village blacksmith. One night a delegation from the blacksmith had come to the house. For hours Li could hear raised voices in her father's hut. She knew something was wrong.

The next morning a violent argument broke out between Sule and his father. Sule denied ever knowing the girl, but Baba wasn't convinced and disowned him. For weeks Sule roamed the village without a home. On several occasions he contemplated suicide but lacked the courage. Li visited him secretly and carried food to him. Li's feelings were confused. What he had done was wrong, yet who was she to urge him into marriage after her own disillusioning experience? Now that Sule had been disowned she could not abandon him, this brother to whom she had always been close.

One day he made up his mind to flee the village and 'enter the world.' Li agreed that this would be best and persuaded Alhaji Bature to help him leave. She missed him very much, however, and retreated still further into her protective shell.

Kaka wept for two days. 'Cursed be me,' he wailed, 'that I should live to see a the day a man-child is disowned for proving his manhood.'

Two months ago, the family of the blacksmith had brought them Sule's child, and now Kaka seemed to live only for his great-grandson.

Jumping up quickly, Li grabbed her charge roughly by the arm. He let out a lusty scream and Awa came running out of Baba's hut.

'Careful Li,' she shouted. 'You are hurting him!'

'By God, you don't want him to crawl into that?' Li pointed to the hearth.

'No, but by God, you need not twist his arm like that. He is only a baby.' Awa fought to control her anger. Her sister was rough with all children including hers, but there was nothing she could do. She could not look after her father and the children as well. She watched as Li dumped the child on the mat and pushed a piece of cassava into his mouth. Kneeling in front of the baby, Li poked her finger into his face.

'Listen little man,' she said. 'If you go that way again, I will break your head.' The child took one look at Li's angry expression and let out a howl, dropping the cassava.

The old man chuckled in his corner. 'Bring the little one here mother,' he called to Li. 'By God, it is hard to choose between you and the hearth. What a fine mother you will make some day!'

'She will not be the same, Kaka' Awa jumped at the chance to put in a bitter word. 'Not after she has had her own.'

Li ignored her. Placing the child, gently this time, on the

old man's lap, she turned to her work and her thoughts. Everybody had changed because of everybody else and Awa was no exception. She was often sullen and unfriendly. Li knew it wasn't just the arrival of the children and Baba's serious illness, but something else that weighed on Awa's mind. Li heard the sound of a motor-bike and turned to peep between the fence. The headmaster and his friend were coming home. Dan Fiama was rarely seen at home these days.

Li remembered a conversation she had overheard some weeks ago. Her neighbours, Mairama and her usual group, had been talking some few paces behind as they all walked to the market.

'Whose daughter is that?' a man from the other side of the river had asked.

'Ah that, she is Baba Garu's daughter.'

'Still at home?' the man asked again.

'Yes, four years waiting for her husband,' Mairama replied, laughing spitefully.

'What kind of husband keeps a bride waiting for four years?' he persisted. 'Either he has got himself a city wife or he is impotent.' The rest laughed.

'I always say strangers are no good, but no one would believe me,' Mairama said.

'You are right, daughter-of-my-mother,' Hauwa joined in.

'And that family will never learn,' Mairama continued. 'Now, they are spreading their bad blood everywhere.'

'Is that true?' the man asked excitedly.

'May I be struck dead if I am lying, but their son has spoilt the daughter of the blacksmith and such a fine woman too.' Mairama confided.

'Eh,' the man grunted with surprise. 'He must marry her then.'

'Not if he is from that family. Instead of doing the right thing, he fled the village.'

'The family is indeed bad,' the man agreed.

'This is only the beginning, my clansman. You have not heard the half of it. And to think that poor Fiama is caught under their thumb!' Mairama shook her head vigorously.

'I heard the older daughter has given him male twins," the man enthused. "She has got the stomach of the pumpkin. The man surely has good luck.'

'Good luck?' Mairama said scornfully. 'I do not call living in that household good luck. Now the poor man cannot even call himself a man among men. What man follows his woman to her home? Today's men have no pride. Sometimes I think our sons are just men for what they have got between their legs.'

'I say it is a bad family that ruins a man's pride,' Manu joined in. 'And I know the cause of all the problems in that family—the old woman. She is a witch!'

Hauwa rose to that. 'Do not blame the woman. She is not a witch but a seer. Just because she accuses several known witches for sucking the blood of her son, you call her one? Tell me, have you heard of a witch attacking other witches openly? I will tell you who the real witch is—she looked at the rest knowingly—the ancient one. They say he uses the shadows of infants to promote the growth of his crops.'

'The woman is right!' A man who was passing by had slowed down to listen to the gossip. 'I have always wondered how a man forty years my senior could harvest more ears of corn than I.'

'Yes, I believe you all,' Manu changed sides. 'They say the evil thing is hidden under the upturned pot at the head of his bed. I've seen it there,' he continued importantly.

'Is that true?' the newcomer asked.

'He should know,' Mairama said impatiently. 'He takes all his meals squatting in front of the ancient one. That's why the old woman hates him.' Manu cowered.

'Unbelievable,' the man from the other side of the river joined in. 'And he so quiet and humble. The world is bad and deceitful. You never know whom to trust.'

'I was never deceived,' Hauwa said. 'No, not by him. That shifty look and crooked smile. You can tell he's not a clean man.'

'Now the gods have caught up with him,' Mairama ventured. 'Nothing is right with that family any more.'

'May the Good Lord save us,' Hauwa said.

'May he save us from the clutches of the wicked ones,' Manu added.

'And may we never be part of it,' concluded the man from

the other side of the river.

At home Kaka had listened intently as Li recounted the conversation to him word for word. When she had finished, he surprised her by bursting into laughter.

'They have to talk, child,' he said simply. 'They have to talk about someone or something and just now our family is ripe for gossip. But do not keep it locked up in your heart. It will swell you up. Bad words are nothing but wasted air. Tomorrow the gossip will shift to another family.'

How right her grandfather had been. Already the villagers were talking about another family whose daughter was carrying an illegitimate child. Li pushed the calabash of groundnuts aside and got up.

'There is a lot of planning to do and decisions to take,' she told herself.

That evening Li went to her grandfather's hut. Lifting the mat that covered the door, she greeted him 'Kaka, did you spend the day well?'

'Come in, my wife, come in, my mother,' he said weakly. Inside, she stood for a while trying to focus her eyes in the semi-darkness. At the corner of the hut a tin lamp burned at its lowest ebb, casting grotesque shadows on the wall. She surveyed the hut carefully, taking in the distinct smell that always reminded her strongly of her grandfather. As she moved, her foot struck against something. She stopped and felt the shape, and finding it strong she sat on it.

Kaka reached out for something under his bed. Shakily, he brought out his pipe and a knotted piece of cloth. Li waited for him patiently as he filled the pipe methodically. He, too, was waiting for Li to broach the subject that had brought her to his hut on a night like this. He drew in the smoke slowly and Li coughed nervously.

'What is it, child?' he asked when Li still did not speak.

'I want to talk with you about something serious,' Li said.

'I am waiting,' he said simply.

She remained quiet for a long time not knowing how to begin. 'I am listening, mother,' he encouraged.

'It is four years now. Four years since the man left us.' Ever since they were formally married, she never referred to Habu by name.

'Yes, child,' Kaka agreed.

'He does not send word any more.' She said with lowered head.

He drew in the smoke deeply and released it.

'He may be busy,' he said without conviction.

'At first I tried to believe it, not any more. He cannot be too busy to send word. I am his responsibility now.' There was no response.

'What am I to do, Kaka?'

'Wait for him child,' he said flatly and Li's heart sank. She had feared this answer.

'Wait for him Kaka?' she said, rather too sharply. 'How long can a woman wait for a man? I am tired and the whole village is laughing behind my back!' A sob rose to her throat.

'Tired of what?' Her grandfather's voice was unexpectedly sharp. Li looked surprised. Not so much by the sharpness of her grandfather's voice but by the realisation that her boredom to escape sprang from many sources. She experienced an intense desire to escape from them all. To run away from the pressure at home, from the constant advances of other men and the mockery in the eyes of the villagers. Could she not run away to a distant place, anywhere with anybody?

Suddenly she felt angry, angry with a man called Habu. Who was he that had married her, opened up the dam of her desire and then left her for years to burn? Truly Habu was nothing. Just another passing stranger, who had come to her when she was ripe for love and deceived her. The villagers were right after all. Habu was a good-for-nothing stranger who wore a tattered shirt and washed out shorts that had lost their seat. Yes, he had fanned the flame of her love, but she was determined to quench its embers.

'You are tired of us!' Grandfather's voice cut her thoughts short.

'No, Kaka,' she protested.

'Yes, child, so you should be. You carry a burden too heavy for your young shoulders. We are old and insensitive and hardly aware of your needs. But be patient. You will soon be free. For now you are the man of the house. Your sister is of great help, but there is so much she has to do with the children around her legs.'

He paused long enough for Li, who chose to be silent. She did not like the trend the conversation was taking.

'Do not worry, mother,' he continued. 'Just be patient. Your father may yet recover by the will of the gods. Your mother's heart is heavy, but she will soon learn to live with her sorrows. As for your demented grandmother and I, we haven't much longer to live.'

'I do not wish to leave you, grandfather.' She uttered a half-truth.

'Learn to be patient,' he repeated. 'You never lose by being patient.'

Li thought, 'I cannot talk about the real reason for my coming now.' Aloud she said, 'May we see the morning,' and made to leave, but her grandfather hadn't finished with her.

'Are there others, child?' he asked and Li was thrown off balance. 'By God, he knows there are others,' she thought desperately, 'to many of whom he has returned gifts himself. Maybe he means in my heart.'

The thought of Alhaji Bature crossed her mind and she smiled to herself. He was a real man with the strength of a lion and the gentleness of a cat. He was considerate and generous like the gods, a man who was the dream of the village maidens. Could she not consent to marry him and live like the daughter-of-a-chief?

Li gave herself a mental shake and stifled a laugh. Alhaji Bature was none of these things. He was a greedy, selfish man who spread his wealth to get what he wanted even at the cost of other people's happiness. He was a cunning, dirty man who showed no interest in a woman until another man did. No, Alhaji Bature was a born hunter who adorned himself with the number of women he acquired.

She raised her head after a long silence. 'No Kaka,' she said a trifle loudly. 'No, there is noone and there isn't going to be any as long as I remain his wife.'

'May the gods of your ancestors bless you child. May they witness this and take it into account,' he said, closing the conversation.

Li got up from her seat and kneeling on both knees said,

'May you sleep well, Kaka, and may we see the light of the morning.'

'Sleep well, child, may we live to see the morning.'

Li sneaked out of the warm hut into a cold dark night. Everything was still. Even the generator had long gone to sleep. An owl suddenly hooted and she shivered involuntarily. 'May the gods protect us from the evil bird,' she said to herself. Half closing her eyes, she dashed to her hut.

Three months later, as the sun was beginning to set, and Li was leaving the house to go to the stream, she ran into a group of men of ripe years, walking slowly in a procession each carrying a bundle under his arm. Without thinking Li dropped the water calabash and rushed back into the house.

'They are here,' she shouted as she brushed past her mother.

Kaka was just coming out of his hut when the visitors salaamed at the gate. On seeing them his face broke into a smile. He moved towards the visitors with all the dignity he could muster. Having clasped hands with each one of them, he showed them in. Shortly afterwards, he came out and called Awa. 'Habu's people are here,' he whispered. 'Ask your husband to come quickly.'

Suddenly, the house became a centre of activities. Mama and the girls got busy in the kitchen. Neighbours who had seen the strange-looking company walk in, started coming, eager to find out the visitors' mission.

Manu was the first to arrive.

'Is it well with the people of this house?' he called out.

'Whom do I welcome?' Li answered as she bent down to feed the fire with more wood.

'It is only your neighbour, Manu.'

'You meet us well, Manu. We have guests.'

'From afar?' he asked Li with a sly grin.

'From afar,' Li answered without looking up.

'They are welcomed if it is good news they bring,' he replied and salaamed at the door. Li's eyes followed him scornfully.

'The whole village will now know that the son of the Mazila clan has strangers from the other side of the river,' she said as Awa walked in.

'Why?' Awa asked.

'The hunchback.'

'That one does not miss a thing in this village.'

'The only thing he'll miss seeing and talking about is his funeral,' Li said and they both laughed. The girls watched as more people walked in and joined the discussion in Kaka's hut.

'Many of them have only come here to fill their stomachs,' Awa said.

'Did you send for the father of the boys?' Li turned to her sister.

'He isn't in his usual place,' Awa replied shortly.

'Just as well,' Li replied. 'If he is drunk he won't be any use in a gathering like this.'

Awa said nothing as she went inside the hut to report to their grandfather. These days she didn't bother to defend Fiama any longer.

Much later, the long discussion in Kaka's hut ended and the old men walked out, belching and grunting with satisfaction.

'Our son's wife is a good cook,' one of the guests commented.

'And her people are very generous,' a neighbour put in.

'May the gods be with your daughter and our son,' said another. 'May the two be as generous as their parents and may they prosper in their generosity.'

'May the wicked ones fall and break their necks as they plotted evil against them.'

'May she have the stomach of the pumpkin.'

'May we live to see the fruits of their union.'

'May they live to carry their children's children and tell stories to them.'

'May they live to bury us.'

'And may their children live to bury them!'

'And may their children's children live to bury their children.' And so it went on.

After the guests left, the villagers went in once more to take a closer look at the gifts they had been brought. Li tried to look indifferent but excitement got the better of her. Twice, she entered the hut on the pretext of collecting dishes.

It was the next morning, however, that Kaka called the

family into the hut to take a look at the gifts — kolanuts, clothes and cosmetics.

Li was told to get ready within a week. Habu's younger brother, Umoru, was to take her to the city. For the next few days, before the great journey, Li lived in a fever of excitement.

Once again she walked with her head held high, her feet barely touching the ground. The news of her journey had already spread in the village. People would stop her on the way to ask when she was leaving and what job her husband did in the city. They would then fish into their pockets or untie the knotted end of their wrappers and bring out money ranging from two pence to two shillings — to aid her on her journey.

At home various food items and household articles, some of which were of no use at all, were brought in. By the end of the week, Li had become a proud owner of articles such as wooden stools, mats, calabashes, clay pots, wire net for smoking meat and fish, stone grinder, traps for catching rats and hoes. The food items were mainly beans, corn, dried meat, smoked fish, groundnuts and dried vegetables.

When Umoru and two other relatives arrived, they took one look at these items and raised strong objections.

'We can't carry all these!' Umoru gestured desperately towards the loads. 'I'll have to hire a lorry just for the loads and I do not have that kind of money.'

But the old women around insisted that every item was important and must be taken. Their daughter would be in a strange city among strange people. Who would lend her anything to use? The boy insisted that the loads were not worth the money he would have to spend to carry them to the city and that many of the articles were useless in the city. But the villagers did not understand. They felt insulted. Who was he to criticise the things they had brought? What had his people brought for her to take? A handful of kolanuts, some pieces of inferior cloth and money that wasn't enough to cover her transport fare.

The heated argument continued for hours until a couple of village elders intervened. Finally it was agreed that Li should take half of the load to the city. The other half should be kept for her at home. Again Li spent some agonising hours, deciding on what to take and what not to take.

At the motor park, as Umoru made negotiations, another problem was encountered. There wasn't enough room for all 'this village junk' said the lorry-mate. Amid insulting laughter, Li's people carted home two-thirds of the load. When everything was settled the bride and her escort sat in the special seats next to the driver of the lorry.

Amid weeping and clasping of hands the lorry set out on its fourteen-hour journey to the city.

# Chapter Seven

The child kicked violently and Li turned on her side. She felt sore and realised she had been lying on one side for far too long. She opened her eyes, wondering what time of night it was. It was hard to tell in the city. The noises of people and vehicles and the bright lights continued long into the night. You slept and woke through them. It was strange for a person who came from a place where only cockcrow signalled the coming of the dawn. She looked at the clock beside her bed. It was only four in the morning.

On the opposite side of the room, Habu lay in a drunken sleep. Li sat on the edge of the bed and regarded her husband thoughtfully. She could see his sad face from the light that came through the window on the side of his bed.

For four years she had yearned to be in her husband's house. She had dreamt of the moments when she would cook his meals, wash his clothes and cuddle him to her breasts. Such moments were rare now. The meals she cooked remained uneaten as his homecomings became later and rarer. And whenever he was at home, the former lion of the village was as unapproachable as an angry god. Li often wondered if Habu had really wanted her to come.

She remembered her first day in the city. After much difficulty in locating the house and the shock of paying a staggering amount of money to transport her load from the motor park to her destination, Li had found an unsmiling welcome awaiting her.

At first she was pleasantly surprised to see the change in Habu. He was much taller and more robust, his clothes were clean and fitted him well. Li felt proud of him but extremely shy in his presence. She longed to talk openly and touch him, but it seemed that Habu wasn't feeling a similar emotion. First he stared at Li unflinchingly as if he had never seen her before, then he turned to his brother and complained loudly about the 'cast offs' from the village. He didn't have enough room to house such 'useless articles'. Li had felt humiliated. A different kind of humiliation from the one she had felt at home in the motor park. She had then accused the laughing lorry-mate of sheer jealousy of another man's bride. Now the man himself had shouted at them for bringing all these 'cast offs'.

Later the same evening, as Li sat in the outer room, Habu and his brother, Umoru, argued heatedly in the bedroom. A few minutes later, Habu came out and brought in an elderly Hausa woman whom he introduced as the 'owner' of the building. He asked the woman to take care of the bride. Li didn't see her husband again until the evening of the next day, by which time Umoru had gone back to the village.

Li served Habu a meal, but he said he wasn't hungry. He looked greatly agitated. She tried talking to him to re-establish the former bond between them, but he remained indifferent. She could still remember clearly that the first time he had desired her was the night he had come home drunk and violent. Even then, Li had found a flicker of happiness in the drunken intimacy.

She bent her head and hot tears trickled down her cheeks. 'Where is my man?' she wailed, silently, 'That boyish man with an incredible smile and a mischevious twinkle in the eye? Where is that proud, self-confident, half-naked lover that defied the laughter of the villagers and walked the length and breadth of the village just to see me?'

Li knew she had lost her man to the city. This man wasn't the man she used to roll with on the sand in front of her father's compound. The man lying on the other side of the room was a well-dressed stranger who did not talk to a village woman. She held her breasts and her sobs stabbed deeper and deeper into her heart.

After some time, she lay on her back and closed her eyes. When she opened them again it was broad daylight and Habu had left for work. She got up, picked up her soap bowl and walked slowly to the single latrine and bathroom combined. The morning rush was over. The men had gone to work and the women were in no hurry to wash. At first the system of queuing up for the bathroom had exasperated Li, but gradually she got used to it. She remembered home, where the woods were a God-given latrine, and the stream a God-given bathroom.

Back in her room, she sat down to an enormous breakfast. Six months pregnant, she had the appetite of a red ant. At the door a voice saluted her and the landlady, whom she had grown to love and respect, entered. She carried herself with an incredible gracefulness that never failed to surprise Li.

'Come in, Hajiya, and let us eat.'

'I will come in but just to talk,' she replied. She sat down in one of the two arm-chairs and they greeted each other.

'You are looking big and well these days,' the woman observed with admiration. Li looked down shyly at her exposed stomach.

'I do my best,' she said. The woman was her mother's age-group and the only confidante she had in the city. Recently, they had taken to telling each other secrets.

'Are you alright?' The woman took a closer look at her young friend. 'You do not sound well.'

'It is the usual problem,' she replied without hesitation.

'Hmmm,' Hajiya grunted. She knew all about Li's problems. 'Don't worry.'

'I try not to, but his attitude is more than I can bear.' She shook her head thoughtfully. 'He does not want me here. I know it now. He treats me as he would treat a dog, with disgust.'

'Do not think like that,' the woman consoled. 'He may have problems in his place of work.'

'You know he hasn't Hajiya. He cannot have had problems for all the months I have been here.'

'Hmmm,' the woman grunted. She always felt uneasy when it comes to this couple's problems. She had never been so closely involved with any tenant before. True, she was often called upon to settle matrimonial quarrels, but somehow she felt committed to this particular couple. She knew more about their problem than they knew. Now she wished she could help her young friend, but instead she felt guilty and responsible. She knew the change in Habu had occurred well before Li came to the city. Li's presence simply made Habu worse. But how could she tell the bride what she knew and what she had seen in this compound with her own eyes? It wasn't possible. Some things that are seen are better left unsaid. Moreover, she would be destroying a home and her duty as a landlady, a friend and a woman with years of marriage experience was to mend and not to destroy.

'The first few years of marriage are often difficult,' she consoled.

'We have been married for five years,' Li replied.

'Yes, but you have been together for only one year.'

'True,' Li agreed, 'but it wasn't like this in the beginning. He was like the son-of-my-mother.'

'Have patience, you have a child on the way. You have something to think about.'

'I don't want to think about the child!' Li answered vehemently. 'What happiness will a child bring that was conceived in drunkeness and silence?'

'May Allah forgive you! Praise be to him, the Merciful. You have no idea how favoured you are.' She paused and shook her head. 'I married at the age of thirteen and for thirty years I prayed . . . for a child. I went to Mecca nine times. I gave all my wealth to mallams, herbalists and spiritual healers for a child that never came. My husband lost no time in marrying other wives who promptly gave him eleven sons and four daughters. I was the eldest wife and the only barren one. With every birth in the family, I experienced a raw agony, but I had to be patient and stay. I was more like an older sister to my husband and a mother to the younger wives. You would have thought I should have a respectable position in the family, but more often than not, I was pushed to the background because I had no child.'

She paused deep in thought. Li was filled with compassion for her. The woman had never said anything to her about her background until now.

'Hajiya, didn't you try the hospital?' she asked, puzzled.

'No child, I do not believe the hospital can give me a child. Birth, like death, is ordained by Allah. A man cannot prevent death from overtaking him by going to the hospital, so, how can he obtain life in the hospital?'

'But Hajiya, I know . . .'

'No child, you do not know. They still would have the child if they hadn't been to the hospital.'

The two remained silent for a long time.

'It is painful and hard when you have no man or child to

hug, but I stayed. I was married to him. It was where Allah wanted me to be. I stayed, Li, not for a year or two, but for thirty years. I may have suffered but in those years I learnt a valuable lesson that patience, as our people always say, does not sour no matter how long you keep it, and a patient person could cook a rock and drink the soup.'

She looked at Li kindly in a motherly manner. 'I want you to be patient and stay, Li. Wait for your man.'

Li closed her eyes and imagined her grandfather's. This gentle woman shared something with her grandfather. Li could not put her finger on it, but whatever it was, it was beautiful. It sustained them and gave them their hold on life.

'Three years ago my husband fell ill,' she was saying and Li opened her eyes. 'He called me to his bedside and gave me some papers. "The building in the heart of the city, behind the Emir's palace is yours. I built it in your name. Keep the papers and as from this month collect the rents. I no longer have the strength to go out and work, and when I die, they will split my wealth over my corpse, like vultures over a carcass. They will not give you a brick because you have no child." That night I wept bitterly for myself and for my husband. All those years I had hugged the idea that he cared only for his children and the mothers of his children. Li, I was gravely mistaken. Deep down in the abyss of his heart, he cared more than I ever knew. A week later, he died and his prediction came true. No one mentioned the barren woman. Later on as they talked about giving the room I was occupying for rent, I packed out of the house to his compound.'

They remained thoughtful for a long time. Finally she raised her head and looked at Li with compassion. 'Your problem is nothing at all. Tomorrow evening we'll go to see someone who can help you!'

Li woke with a start and saw her husband standing by her bedside, a worried look on his face. 'I woke you up,' he explained. 'You were having a nightmare.' She got up slowly and sat at the edge of the bed until her trembling subsided. The dream had been as vivid as if it were real.

She had been sent for by her mother. On reaching the

village, she found her ancestral home deserted and all the huts in a state of ruin. Some of the walls were crumbling, others had their roofs and doors caved in. Bushes had grown around the compound and it was almost impassible. Wall geckos and spiders assailed her as she tried to go further in. She called but not a single person was there. Although the huts were in ruin, all were still standing except for her father's. She moved to the spot where her father's hut had once been and saw a heap of red soil. Li raised a heart-rending wail which Habu heard as a deep agonising groan.

'Man,' she spoke to her husband who had gone back to bed. 'Hmmm?'

'I want to go home and see my parents.'

'Was the nightmare about going home?'

'No!'

'You can't travel in your state,' he said firmly. Li was now well into her eighth month.

'Yes, I can,' Li insisted stubbornly.

'No, you cannot and you will not.' He pulled his bedclothes over his head.

'Please man, I will . . .'

'Go to sleep, woman, or let me sleep. I have to go to work tomorrow.'

'Then I will prepare to go home,' Li said sulkily.

'Do what you like, but if you go, just remember not to come back to this house,' he said irritably.

'I will remember that very well,' she retorted, 'but just you remember to give me my divorce paper!'

He said nothing to that.

'If you call yourself a man, divorce me properly!' Li was warming up for a real quarrel, but Habu wasn't ready for it. He sank further into his bedclothes. Li jumped out of bed and removed the clothes from over his head.

'Why don't you say something like a real man? Why do you hide your face in silence?'

'Why don't you shut your mouth?' he said vehemently.

'Come and shut it for me,' she shouted. 'I didn't know until now that I married a coward from an unworthy clan.'

'Keep my clan out of this,' he glared at her.

'If you have any respect for your ancestors you had better

divorce me properly. I will not go home and wait for you,' she fumed. 'Li, daughter of the Mazila clan, waits for no man. There are worthier men around than you.'

'You leave me alone!' He sat up and pointed a warning finger at her.

'Yes, you leave alone,' she mimicked. 'That's all you're good for, leaving alone. What would you do if I did not? Kill me?' She stood right in front of him and dared him to touch her.

'I could do just that', he shook with suppressed anger.

'Then do it, you coward,' she blazed at him. 'Show that you are a man with a heart.' By now Habu had managed to scramble into his clothes inspite of the enormous size that blocked his way. On seeing that her husband intended to flee from the house, she blocked the inner door with her body.

'You'll have to kill me first to pass,' she shouted. Habu pushed her aside gently and as he put on his shoes to leave, Li heaped curses on him. 'Shame, shame, shame on you,' she yelled, 'May the gods punish you!'

She felt cheated and humiliated and could not contain the bitter tears that stung her eyes. She lay on her bed and cried until sleep overcame her.

That day Habu did not come home until late in the night. Li pretended sleep. Henceforth the two maintained a sullen silence between them. She felt it would be a disgrace to go back to the village just yet, for what would the villagers who fed fat on gossips think? Gradually, she pushed the quarrel and the urge to go home to the back of her mind.

But a fortnight later, as she was having a bath, the land-lady's voice jolted her.

'You have a visitor from the village. He said he is the brother of your father.' All her fears came back as she dashed out of the bathroom, her heart thumping wildly.

'Take care,' the woman cautioned as Li rushed past her. 'He isn't going to turn right back to the village,' she teased.

At the gate, Li stood for a moment and stared at her uncle, her eyes wide with fear. She searched his eyes for a sign of bad news. Finding none, she welcomed him and led him into the house. She was glad to see someone from home, but his unexpected arrival filled her with foreboding.

After the old man had eaten and belched with satisfaction

he told her his mission.

'Is it only illness, father?' she asked anxiously.

'I would not have come myself if it were something else.'

They both avoided the one dreadful word. Li still did not believe him. The dream she had a few weeks before now printed itself on her memory with a certain force of reality all its own.

'Your father was moved to the hospital weeks ago when he seemed to be in such pain. Then in the hospital he closed his eyes for days and did not open them again until the day before yesterday. For the first time in weeks, he spoke. He asked about you and Sule. "Where is my son?" he murmured. 'I have something to say to my son.' Then he paused for a long time. We were about to move away when your grandfather noticed his lips moving. He moved forward and bent over your father. "Send for Li to come. She knows where my son is," he said and went to sleep. After he spoke his breathing became much easier and his expression more peaceful. We all believe it is a sign of recovery. Yesterday your grandfather sent me to fetch you, and to ask you about Sule's whereabouts. In the city you may have heard some news of him?'

Li sighed and shook her head sadly. She hoped her uncle had spoken the truth. If her presence would be of any help to her father, she was ready to go home. But somehow, deep down in her heart, she knew her father had no need of anybody's presence but that of his ancestors. His hut was already in a shambles.

The next morning, Li and her uncle stood by the gate to Garba's compound in Kano. It was still early in the morning. The journey to Kano had taken only two hours. Li was eager to go straight home but Habu had cautioned her uncle against a tiring journey. 'Garba will keep you in Kano for the night,' he had said, 'and tomorrow at dawn you can set out for the village.' It wasn't such a bad idea after all.

Li was looking forward to seeing Faku, whom she had not seen for almost six years. She wondered how Faku would look after all these years. Fat? Modern looking? Rich and sophisticatead? Li had learnt, from Faku's mother in the village, that Garba had another woman with six children. How did they all live?

A little boy came out and asked them to follow him. Li dragged herself in, while her uncle remained in the outer room with their luggage. The boy, who Li guessed was Faku's son, led her into a room. Li removed her slippers at the door, saluted and entered. She stood still at the entrance and stared at the gaunt-looking woman before her. For a brief second, she thought she was in the wrong room. The gaunt woman rose slowly from the mat where she was sitting and advanced doubtfully towards Li. She, too, was obviously unsure. But as she drew nearer, she recognised Li and smiled openly. Li's face lit up as she rushed into Faku's open arms. 'Faku!' she wailed. 'Faku my friend.'

Li had recognised Faku as soon as she smiled, revealing the once beautiful dimples, now wider and deeply set into a thin haggard face. They clung to each other and sobbed for a long time. At last Faku led her to a mat.

'Daughter-of-my-mother,' Faku finally said, wiping the tears from her eyes. 'Forgive me. That was a poor welcome for your tired body.'

'By God, you are not to blame, my mother, daughter-of-the-chief.' Li addressed her in terms of endearment. 'Both of us were overcome.'

'We should be dancing for joy, not sobbing,' said Faku, blowing her nose into the end of her wrapper.

'Sobbing is another way of expressing happiness,' Li said.

Faku got up and went into the inner room, emerging with a covered bowl. 'I'm told a man accompanies you?' she asked.

'Yes, the brother-of-my-father. He is in the outer courtyard.'

'I will go and welcome him.'

Faku walked out and Li watched her go. She could not believe this was reality. How could this near-stranger be her friend Faku? Famished in body and no doubt famished in soul? The house was filled with tiny feet, running in and out of the outer room, but no feet came into Faku's room. She looked round the tiny outer room. There wasn't much in it, two old arm-chairs, a small wooden table, some tattered mats and a half-filled glass cupboard. She heard approaching footsteps and raised her head. A fat woman, holding a small girl's hand and carrying a smaller one astride her hips, saluted Li at the door and entered.

'Welcome stranger, did you travel well?'

Li knew instantly this must be Faku's co-mate.

'Thank-you, mother-of-the-house; do I find you well?'

'Well, thanks to Allah the Great. You must be Li.'

'Yes, mother-of-the-house, you know the name well.'

'I do. Faku talks a lot about you and another sister she calls Awa. She says you are the only sisters she has.'

'True,' Li answered coolly.

'Who is the older?' the woman asked.

'Awa,' Li said and hoped the questions would end there. She had started lying just to support her friend. In a polygamous home, the number of relatives a woman has is important, so is her background.

'I see.' The woman smiled and revealed a gold tooth in the upper row. 'She has been to Mecca too,' Li thought. She sensed something she didn't like about the woman, but could not tell immediately. Something about her eyes, probing, or was it the intimidating way she asked questions?

'How long are you staying with us?' she asked Li.

'Until tomorrow.'

'So soon?' the woman smiled incredulously.

'Yes, our father is ill,' Li replied.

'Ah, may Allah give him health. Faku did not tell me about this.'

'She does not know,' Li answered.

'She too is going home then?' she persisted and Li cursed inwardly. They both heard Faku's footsteps coming and the woman backed out.

'Rest well, stranger,' she called outside.

'Thank-you, mother-of-the-house.'

Faku exchanged greetings with the woman outside and entered.

'She came to salute you?' she asked anxiously.

'Yes. She is the mother of the house?'

'Yes,' Faku replied flatly. 'You have to pay back the visit in the evening.'

'I will,' Li promised.


Much later, they sat on the mat and talked over the past. Both avoided talking about the present as if it didn't matter to either of them, until Li tired of the pretence.

'Daughter-of-my-mother, you have changed.'

'So have you, Li,' she replied defensively.

'You used to be the fat one and I, the thin one,' Li persisted.

'Things have changed.'

'Yes, what has happened? Are you happy, Faku?' She looked at her friend closely. 'Is he kind to you?'

'Yes.' The reply was curt.

'Our people believe happiness shows itself in the flesh and the face of a person tells the story of their soul,' Li said seriously.

'Our people must be right, but there must be other ways of showing the state of mind. Remember, some people grow fat on unhappiness,' Faku said.

Li was silent for a long time. Then she said sullenly, 'How true, daughter-of-my-mother. I ought to know that very well.'

'No, Li!' Faku was a little ashamed at what she had said. 'Yours is a healthy fatness.'

'Mine is a foolish fatness,' Li replied. 'How is Garba?' she asked, changing the subject.

'I don't know,' Faku replied. 'I don't see him often.'

'Does he travel a lot?'

'Always. He says he is a businessman. What kind of business he does I do not know. His wife ought to know. Twenty years is long enough to find out.'

'Have they been married that long?'

'That long and nine children between them. She is the mother-of-the-house and the master of the house too.' Faku's voice dropped and Li felt sorry for her friend. Li had felt cold and lonely, but here was someone who she sensed felt much colder and lonelier.

'But you have your little boy?' Li asked and Faku's face lit up.

'I was beginning to wonder if you had forgotten him. He is not so little any more. You saw him earlier on today. He it was who brought you in.'

'I thought so. He has your looks.'

They talked far into the night, but Faku told her friend little about her life as Garba's second wife.

That night, Li had a strange dream. She was outside Faku's

outer room, peering in through a half-open window. She saw Faku, naked, standing in the middle of the room. Looking round, Li observed that the room was bare also. She was about to speak to Faku when she suddenly noticed Garba leaving the room. Li watched as he banged the door after him. He walked straight without turning back and Li was surprised to see the door of a new building open in front of him. He entered the building and the door closed slowly behind him.

Li woke up, disturbed, but soon fell asleep again. This time she was crossing a desert land and saw from a distance the shape of a woman tilling the land. As she moved closer, the shape became that of Faku. She tilled with all her strength, but the land was dry and remained unyielding. The dust that rose enveloped her until she was one with the earth. Li stopped and watched her for some time. At last she said, 'The land is no good, Faku. It is barren. You are wasting your energy for nothing.' But Faku did not pay attention to her. She continued to till desperately. Li turned and left her friend still tilling.

In the morning, as Li prepared to leave for the village, she asked her friend once more if she had told her everything about her marriage and if she was truly happy.

'By God, I am enjoying my life in the city! Isn't the city what you and I always wanted, daughter-of-my-mother?' Faku said vehemently.

'By my ancestors, yes, but I am talking about you, not the city,' Li replied.

Faku avoided her friend's eyes.

'I hope everything is what you hoped for?' Li repeated.

'Don't worry about me, Li. I am all right. Go to the village, and when you get there, say this for me to my mother. The land is still brown and unyielding. Not until it is covered with green will I come to the village.'

Li stared at her with an unfathomable expression, but Faku simply laughed.

'Don't look like that, Li,' she said to prevent Li from further probing. 'Just tell her that. My mother will understand.'

'I will,' Li promised.

'Go well then, friend, and I pray you find your father in better health.'

But even as they bade each other farewell, the mourners at home were beginning to disperse.

# Chapter Eight

A young woman of twenty-nine walked round her dead father's compound deep in thought. She was recalling a dream she had had years ago. Climbing the heap of soil that had once been her father's hut, she turned to look at the rest of the dilapidated huts. From where she stood, she could see the ancient one crouched among the dead ashes of the fire hearth, his pregnant goat bleating at his side. Kaka had made a desperate attempt to cover a collapsed portion of the hut with an old mat, without success.

'A house without a man,' Li wailed inwardly. 'Where is Sule, son-of-my-mother?'

She shook her head sadly at the dilapidated huts, as she climbed down the heap of soil and entered her grandfather's hut. She greeted him, but the ancient one was sullen and in no mood to talk. Li left for the hut opposite his. The old woman lay entangled in a pile of worn-out blankets which had gone stiff and brittle with age and dirt. She heard Li's footsteps and grumbled loudly about the cruel weather and unsympathetic people. Li knelt down to rekindle the fire in the hearth. Having done that, she dashed out as the smell in the hut became overpowering.

Outside, she breathed freely again. Surveying the compound once more, she made a mental picture of what she intended to do with it after she had completed her course at the Advanced Teachers' college. A mighty modern building to house everybody, old and young. A regular monthly income to educate the small ones and keep the old ones warm and well-fed. Such had been her ambitions when she had fled the village five years ago. But Awa's urgent letter had been the reason for her return to the village before her goals had been reached.

'Come home, daughter-of-my-mother, and see for yourself,' it read. 'Our father's compound is in ruins. There is not a single man around. Kaka's eyes have failed him and the HM has lost his head in the bottles.'

Li was now home to 'see for herself.' She could not forget the last time she had been at home and the reasons for her flight from the village. Li cringed with shame at the memory.

After her father's death and the birth of her daughter, Shuwa, Li had waited to be fetched by her husband as the custom demanded. Habu neither came to console the family nor to acknowledge the birth of their firstborn. After two years with no word from her husband, new and old suitors began to flock round Li, chief among them Alhaji Bature. Once more her name began to be linked with his; once more the village started to gossip. This time Li refused to be disturbed in spite of her family's silent disapproval.

One night Awa begged her to go back to the city, to her husband. 'The village is laughing behind our backs once more. Take heart and go back to your husband. No one needs know he did not send for you.' But Li would not hear of this. 'May the gods forbid it!' She clapped her hands in Awa's face to indicate her indignation at the suggestion. 'It is not done, daughter-of-my-mother. The day a woman begins to woo a man has not yet come and if it has, it will not begin with me.'

And then, when her child was exactly two years old and weaned, Alhaji Bature started to woo her openly, in spite of Kaka's furious protests and Mama's undisguised fears. Mama warned that Li was still married and the trader's actions would eventually plunge the family into disgrace.

At first Li laughed at all of them. 'If there is a man left in Habu's family, let him come out and challenge the trader. What kind of lame family am I married into?'

In fact she felt greatly flattered that she could still command a man's attention after Habu's rejection. She began to dress extravagantly and to frequent cultural dances and festivals. The flow of suitors increased and her name began to come easily to men's lips. She had reached the peak of her womanhood and was overwhelmed by her own popularity. Everybody could see the direction Li was heading except her; in her new glory she was oblivious to everything.

Then one morning Li went to the stream to fetch some water. On reaching the stream she met a lot of women queuing up to use a single sand-well. Thinking how lazy and stupid they were not to dig another well, Li moved a few yards away and dug a large well. Having done that she went to fetch her water-jar. On coming back to her new well, she was surprised to find that half the women who had been waiting to take water from the other well were now queuing up at her well. She pushed through the throng, demanding to fill her water-jar first, but they pushed her back.

'You join the queue!' a young woman glared at her. 'Can't you see we are all waiting?'

'But I dug the well!' Li looked from one face to another quite bewildered. None of the women answered her.

'You saw me dig that well!' she pointed out, infuriated at the injustice of it all.

'You dug the well, so what?' said a young woman.

'So I get to fill my jar first,' she stressed, but the women broke into laughter.

'No!' they chorused.

'It doesn't always work that way,' the young woman who spoke first said. 'This well is common property, dug by one but to be used by all.' They all burst out laughing again.

Li was puzzled. She did not know what they were getting at. Of course wells were common property. It was dug by one person but used by all, but there was a common understanding, an unwritten law, that the person who dug the well used it first. Why were the women hostile to her? She looked from one woman to another. Two or three were known to her, the rest of the faces were vaguely familiar.

'Does it hurt so much to share, Li?' one of the known ones said to her. 'You are not the only one who knows how to use other people's things, so you must learn to share as we do.'

'Yes, queen of the village, the sooner you learn the better,' another woman put in.

It was then Li became aware of what was happening. She recognised two of the women as wives of her ardent admirers. For a moment she lost her composure.

A dreadful fear crept into her eyes, and engulfed her whole being. Her body became cold and she could hardly hold her jar. She made to back out, but already a circle was forming around her. The insults increased. Some of the women threatened to beat her. Others suggested stripping her.

'Let's have a look at what our men are dying for!' said

one rather fat woman.

'Yes, let's do that!' the rest agreed excitedly. One of them jumped at Li and snatched her scarf and the rest applauded. As a second attempt was being made to remove her wrapper, an old man, owner of a cassava farm nearby, appeared at the bank of the stream. The circle broke up immediately.

Li snatched at her jar and her scarf, which was thrown at her, and ran towards the old man. As she was running away, insults followed her: 'Unsaddled horse!' 'The vulture that isn't anybody's chicken!' 'Rich man's plaything!'

That day, Li wept inconsolably, but the worst was yet to come. A week after the incident, Li's name was carried maliciously to the dancing arena.

Henceforth she remained at home and could not venture out for shame. But how long was she to remain a prisoner at home? She re-examined her position and decided her days were over in the village. But where was she to go? Awa and her mother pressed her to return to her husband, but Kaka begged her to wait at home.

'It isn't done,' he kept on saying. 'The spirit of your father will not forgive me. Let the man give us our due respect.'

Li wouldn't listen to any of these suggestions. All these years she had waited for a man who cared nothing about her. Was it not obvious, right from the beginning, that he had lost interest in her? Was she to spend the rest of her life waiting for a man like a dog waiting for the bone from its master's plate? Who says a husband makes for a guardian or a father? Certainly not the Hausas, who would say, "A woman who takes a husband for a father will die an orphan."

She had then vowed to go back into the world and make an independent life for herself. Dusting her class seven certificate, she had fled from the village, leaving her daughter behind.

Now five years later, she was ready to read for her Advanced Teachers' Certificate. She intended to be the most educated woman in the village and for miles around. Only then would she assume the role of the 'man of the house' in her father's compound.

Li shook her head once more at the dilapidated huts and went inside one of them, where Awa was cutting some fresh vegetables for the evening meal. Li sat down and watched the children play around the hearth. Like Mama, Awa was contributing generously to the population of the village. She had a child every other year including a set of twins. On the day Li arrived, she had felt drowned in the midst of children.

'Big sister,' she had commented. 'This place looks like the house of the chief.' 'Of course it does,' Awa had answered mockingly. 'It is the house of the chief alcoholic.'

'You have the womb of the pumpkin,' Li had continued.

'Do not forget other people's contribution, including yours,' Awa had replied.

Shuwa, now seven years old, walked in with a calabash full of water.

'Ma,' she said to Awa, 'the well water is muddy. Can Gambo and I go to the stream?' Gambo, the girl born after the twins was two years older than Shuwa. The two were inseparable. 'No, my mother,' Awa said tenderly. 'You can go tomorrow morning. It is getting late now.'

'We want to go now, mother,' Shuwa insisted with a defiant look in her eyes.

'I say NO,' Awa replied firmly, 'and get out of here. I want to talk with your mother.' Shuwa shot out like an arrow and Li smiled after her.

'She is every drop you,' Awa commented.

Li shook her head doubtfully. 'She does not look like me at all.'

'True. She looks like her father, from the shape of her head to that of her toes, but she resembles you in character. She is as restless as a goat in labour, as stubborn as a tired donkey and as arrogant as a dethroned chief.'

'Big sister,' Li protested, laughing, 'that bit surely isn't me.'

'No,' Awa smiled. 'It is not possible to divide up a child. A child is a combination of both parents. That is why, Li, a marriage with a child in it has to remain intact. Break up a home and it is the child you are breaking.'

'I hope you have never said anything to her about her father?' Li asked anxiously.

'You need not worry, daughter-of-my-mother. Shuwa, like the rest of the children in this house, asks no questions. For them there is only one father, Kaka. The HM is just some drunken fool who comes home from time to time to harass their mother for drink-money.'

Awa looked at her sister and Li shook her head silently. 'What changed your man, big sister? He used to be the best there was in the village. I hope our father's house was not the cause. It is an unlucky family, where "even the she-goat gives birth to a dog".'

'I don't know, Li, but I think many things helped to change my man. The village itself changed and he changed with it. The government took over the mission school just as we had hoped. A secondary school was added to it. But it wasn't my man they made head over the school. They said he wasn't educated enough to head such a big school, so a stranger was brought to take his place. This time a brown man. He wasn't even white, Li. Not the white people we are used to in the village. My man was pushed into the junior classes to teach. Those of us that could barely read were asked to work anywhere in the school except the classrooms. The men have no choice. Most of them have grown too stiff in the waist to till their ancestral lands, so, they were content to sweep the offices and run errands, jobs their women and small children do at home.'

Awa paused for a minute and looked at her sister. 'I had a choice Li, the children and the old people at home, so I left. I didn't have to stay and be humiliated by other people's children. My husband had to stay. We needed the money. He stayed, but it wasn't to feed the children. You know now where his money goes. I wouldn't have known how to cope without Mama. We live on the proceeds of her farm. The woman would go to the farm at cockcrow and won't come back until the chickens have gone to roost!'

Li listened silently, feeling guilty. She had done nothing herself but add to the growing number of mouths . . .

Awa sensed her uneasiness and said, 'Alhaji Bature has helped a lot these past years, on your behalf.'

Li made as if to pounce on her sister. 'Big sister, you cannot mean that.'

'It is true, Li,' Awa looked at her pleadingly. 'I cannot help it when he comes well-stocked with food and the children are hungry. I haven't the heart. And if it gives him pleasure to feed us for your sake, why should I refuse him? Moreover the man is destined for you by the gods. Forget the other man. The villagers were right after all. He is no good for you.'

'How can I forget the father of my child, big sister? You yourself said just now that to break up a home is like breaking a child.'

'True, but isn't your home broken already? Is the child living with either of you? This is her home. She does not know any other home, so don't bring the child into this. As for being the father of your child, you are indeed speaking like a child. If he can forget the mother of his child, why can't you forget him? He did not even sympathise with us in our grief. And the child, does he even know he has a child, Li?'

Awa paused to look closely at her sister. Li said nothing. 'He isn't a real man, Li, and from the rumours I heard recently, he is even less of a man now.'

Li checked an angry retort. What right had Awa to talk like that?

'Child, forget the man,' Awa continued, now like a mother. 'He is not the type a woman waits for. The gods must have sent him as an escort to accompany real men. Look, we have done nothing for Alhaji Bature, yet the man would go to war for us. What more do you want from a man?'

'Nothing, big sister,' Li replied after a pause. 'I don't want anything.'

'Then marry him. All our problems would be over,' she said, and Li thought, 'While mine begin.' Aloud she said, 'I will marry no one. What do I want a man for?'

'Every woman needs a man,' Awa insisted, 'at least to mend the fence,' she added.

'Not me.'

'Even you and your daughter too.'

'I am all the father she will ever have,' Li declared.

Awa sighed. 'The city has changed you.'

'No, not the city. I hardly knew the city.'

'He changed you then?'

Li nodded. She was remembering the day the truth first began to dawn on her. It was the day Hajiya the landlady, took her to see the man she said would help her. The man had turned out to be a spiritualist.

He was praying when they entered. They sat quietly in a corner and waited. When he had finished, he reached out for a big tray full of fine sand. Without saying a word to them, he scribbled on the dust and erased it. Then he asked Li to place five shillings beside the tray, and press her right hand, palm down, on the sand. Li did so, and he levelled the sand and scribbled some more. He contemplated the writing for a long time and finally nodded his head in a gesture of contentment.

'I know why you are here,' he said. 'You are heavy in two places. Heavy in body and heavy in mind.' Li listened quietly not totally convinced of his wisdom.

'I see problems ahead,' he studied the scribble again. 'You have to work very hard to ward off the evil that hangs over your marriage.' He smiled smugly and Li wondered what it was he was savouring. 'Look, I can see your husband's back towards you and that is a bad sign. There is also a woman between the two of you, tall and fair in looks. You will have to work on her before she destroys your home.' Li nodded silently. 'I have a special medicine here. I give it only to people in genuine distress like you. I do not give it to women who want to snatch other people's husbands. I work for the welfare of marriage.'

The landlady nodded in agreement, murmuring favourable comments but Li took it all in silently.

'Come back in three days to give me time to put the medicine together,' he concluded.

Li and the landlady had returned three days later to collect the medicine. There were three amulets. 'This one,' the man had said, handing Li the small rectangular object, 'is to be sewn into your man's pillow. It is to ensure that he thinks of you all the time.' The second amulet was to be thrown into a pit latrine. 'This will ensure that your husband, henceforth, will look with contempt on the other woman, just like the thing that goes down the pit.' The third amulet which looked peculiar in shape, was to be buried in a graveyard. 'Henceforth peace and quiet will reign in your home.'

Li had paid a staggering amount of money for the treatment. Outside the man's house, she had turned to the landlady, 'I don't believe him, Hajiya, all this talk about another woman!'

'Li,' the landlady had said sharply. 'If the man said there is another woman, then there is. I believe every word he said. Just do exactly as he had said and there will be no problem.' The instructions given were carried out meticulously, but there was no improvement. With the landlady's encouragement, Li visited the man several times and paid more money.

The miracle did not take place. Li, although cynical right from the beginning, continued to spend her savings out of sheer desperation.

It was long after, when she was far away from it all, that everything began to fall into place. The landlady's remarks here and there began to be significant. She had known a lot of things about Habu that Li would never know. The visit to the spiritualist was no doubt the woman's attempt to open Li's eyes to the cause of her problems without causing too much harm. But Li's money went and her eyes remained stubbornly closed, until years later, when Habu's younger brother started writing desperate letters.

'Come back, our wife,' he had written. 'There is a witch-like woman in the house ruining your husband's life. She moved in a few months after you left.' Li never replied to the boy's letters, but he continued to write, filling her in with the news of her husband and the woman.

'Habu's parents are troubled,' Awa cut into her thoughts. 'They have been to see grandfather five times since you left.' Awa paused for a minute, then added, 'The last time they came, they brought two live chickens!' Awa suppressed a giggle but Li burst out laughing.

'You can see how much I am worth, daughter of my mother, two live chickens!'

'How about Habu?' Awa asked more seriously. 'Did he attempt to see you at any time since you left him in the city?'

'He came to the school twice to plead with me to go back. He also sent friends.'

'The scoundrel,' Awa hissed. 'Is that how to bring back a wife? Does he not know the way to the village any more?'

'Maybe it's the city way,' Li said sarcastically.

'Did he marry you in the city?'

'I asked him if he had been to see the people at home. He

replied that he was too ashamed to face them. What could he say if he went back to the village?'

'The fool,' Awa said again. 'So he should be. Did he ask about the child?'

'He begged to see just a picture of her.'

'And what did you say?' Awa asked anxiously.

'No. So he asked if the child knew he was her father.'

'Yes?' Awa prompted.

'I told him there is more to being a father than lying between a woman's thighs.'

Awa clapped her hands like a little girl. 'You are beginning to get sense into your head, daughter-of-my-mother. Indeed you are.'

'He wept that day,' Li said sadly, as if the memory pained her. 'The second time he came, so smartly dressed you wouldn't recognise him, he told me everything about him and the city woman.'

On hearing this, Awa moved her stool closer to her sister.

'She came from the south. They worked in the same office. It was when Habu was new in the city and was a bit awkward, but she showed him round, cooked for him and was generally helpful. The friendship went too far and she found herself with child. She could not have the baby. She was living with her uncle and if he found out, he would have killed her. She had to commit abortion or suicide. There was no other choice. Habu found a herbalist. A large sum of money was paid. Money borrowed from the unsuspecting landlady. Three days later, the same landlady was hurried into Habu's room. A woman was unconscious in a pool of blood. From there, there was no hiding anything. The hospital. Her uncle. An operation. She lost both the baby and the baby bag. Habu was given a choice between a court action and a forced marriage. He picked the latter. Three years later, I went to the city, so the pattern of his life changed. He rented a room for her at the other end of the town and his double life began. Late nights, unscheduled journeys and bitter silences. When I left the city, the woman moved in again.'

Awa simply looked at her sister dumbfounded. 'By God,' she whispered. 'By God and you kept all this to yourself, Li? Of course we heard rumours, but it was nothing like what you have told me. Why didn't you talk?'

'What was the point of stripping him naked in the village? Already I was laughed at for marrying a heartless stranger. Should I offer more food for their wagging tongues? We all have problems, daughter-of-my-mother, but the secret is to keep it from prying eyes.'

'You are a bigger fool than I thought and your husband a coward of the worst type. Now tell me. What did he want with you if he has a woman?'

'He was unhappy, he said, and wanted me and the child back. I refused. He begged and said we needed each other to survive, but I told him we did not want him or need him. For years we had survived without him, we could do so again and again. That day he knelt and placed his head on my thighs. Clasping my legs with both hands he cried, big sister, cried the way I have never seen a man cry before. "What am I to do?" he wailed. "I am ruined. I will commit suicide if you do not come back." But with every drop of tears, my heart hardened. I could not forget the way he had ignored me in the city, a village woman. At last he wiped his eyes and looked at me. "You are still my woman," he said childishly. "No," I replied. "Not any more. I stopped being your wife a long time ago. For me, Habu, you have ceased to exist." Daughter-of-my-mother, he raised his tear-stained face and I can never forget the look in his eyes. Slowly he got up, reached for the key to his company car, and went out. After that, he did not come any more. A year after his visit, Garba came to our school. I was busy preparing for my examinations, so he stayed only for a short time. He told me about the accident.'

'Yes, the accident. We heard only rumours. How bad was it?' Awa asked more from curiosity than concern.

'Very bad, it was a company car and there were five people in it including the driver. All were killed except Habu who escaped but with badly crushed legs.'

'What happened?'

'A collision with an oncoming trailer over a bridge.'

'My ancestors!' Awa wailed. 'Will Habu ever walk again?'

'It is still hard to say. They sent for me immediately after the accident. I stayed until he was out of danger. But he is still in hospital. It seems as though he has lost the will to live.

The doctors say they have done everything that they can, and that the rest depends on him.'

'Hmm,' Awa grunted, giving her sister a sidelong look. 'Why must you worry yourself about him? There is his woman to take care of him.'

'No, big sister. She left.'

'She left?' Awa paused in silent amazement. 'She has more sense than you,' she said finally. 'That woman from the south has no use for leftovers.'

'Don't talk like that, big sister,' Li protested.

'It is the truth, isn't it? You are only called in to collect the pieces, daughter-of-my-mother. Put him together again and she or someone else will come along and snatch him away from you. You will be the loser all over again.'

'She is the loser, not me. Remember, she too is crippled, what does she need another cripple for? True, I lost my man to her and at first I was bitter, but gradually I learnt to accept my fate. She wasn't to blame. This is a game of life and we are all struggling to survive. The woman from the south is no exception. Now I feel sorry for her because I have, at least, my child to remind me of those moments we had together. The poor woman has nothing to show for those years. Nothing at all, just an aching emptiness.'

'I do not understand you, daughter-of-my-mother. You have grown incredibly soft.' Awa shook her head.

'And you big sister, surprisingly hard.'

'It is the way of life,' Awa said sadly. 'Do you remember when we were girls? Our dreams? None of our dreams seem to have come true, not even for Faku. I learnt the world has collapsed on her head.'

'So I heard,' Li replied, 'but no one can tell me the truth of what had happened. Garba would not talk for bitterness and her mother keeps a sullen silence.'

'I heard she has left Kano for some other town and is deep in prostitution,' Awa pursued.

'So they told me, big sister,' Li replied reluctantly. 'Who knows the truth.'

'Apparently the first wife made medicine to make her barren and was busy making another one to drive her insane, so she ran away.'

Li looked at her sister disapprovingly. 'Don't believe all you hear, big sister. The village is full of wild rumours. Like all of us, Faku has her problems and is struggling the best way she can to survive. The method she chose should not concern anybody else.'

Awa looked at her sister with amazement. She opened her mouth to speak but closed it again. Li had changed incredibly. This wasn't the sister she was used to, impetuous and critical of people. This was a different Li, tolerant and understanding. What had brought about this change? The emotional hardships she went through—the city? If the city could change Li, then the city could not be all bad, thought Awa who had never been there. Li had, no doubt, matured and in the process of maturing had become a better person with a finer soul.

'Is the city so bad then?' asked Awa.

'More than you think, big sister. It destroys dreams.'

After the evening meal, Li went out into the streets and marvelled at the change in the village. The main street was lighted by the numerous kerosene lamps and mini gas generators from rich houses. She moved slowly among the throng of busy people, hawkers of all kinds of wares, idlers and streetwalkers. On each side of the street, shops, kiosks and stalls were springing up. Li also observed with sadness that the front yards of elders and ward heads, that used to serve as recreation centres for yelling children, were now commercial centres for petty traders. The days of dancing, singing and holding hands under the watchful eyes of the full moon were over.

Earlier on in the day, she had observed with awe that there was no longer any distinction between the Hill Station and the African quarters. With new zinc houses springing up everywhere, the two places had merged into one solid piece of metal. She could not conceal her dismay at the total disappearance of the backyard gardens, displaced by these new constructions.

At dawn, there was no sound of the cockcrow. Early in the morning, no one came to wake you up with the latest gossip. Everybody kept himself to himself. Li grieved inwardly. Awa was right after all, when she had said, 'We needn't go to the city, the city will come to us.'

# Chapter Nine

Li's eyelid began to twitch. She placed a finger on the spot. The twitching had been going on for a week, but nothing had happened. 'Could it be that my eyes are just tired of reading?' she asked herself as she walked back to the women's hostel. But she knew it wasn't just reading. It was the usual omen that an important visitor was on the way.

It was Li's final year at the Advanced Teachers' College. In another week, the final examinations that would transform Li into a highly qualified teacher would begin. Already she had washed and packed her things in readiness for the journey back to the village. Yes, she still thought of her home town as 'the village.' She walked jauntily without thinking or looking at where she was going.

'As-s-ha-a!' Li let out a yell, as she knocked her big toe against a jutting stone, stumbled and nearly fell over a chameleon. 'Gods of my ancestors,' she exclaimed excitedly. 'First the twitch, then my big toe and a chameleon crossing my path. Maybe I will get a visit from one of my ancestors.'

Nothing happened that day or the next. But on the third day, Li woke in the morning with a heavy feeling. She was highly irritable and did not greet anybody as she got ready to go to school. Suddenly someone knocked loudly at her door. Li refused to answer hoping that whoever was at the door would soon give up. But the person had his mind set. The knocking got louder and louder.

'Stop knocking so loudly,' Li shouted nervously and flung the door open. The security man in his gaudy uniform stood there at attention. 'Ah,' it is you, Baba Maigadi,' Li said with undisguised relief.

'Yes, Misi,' he answered, still standing erect.

'Why were you knocking so loudly?' Li asked.

'To wake you up, Misi. A man outside swore he must see you, Misi.'

'What man outside, Baba Maigadi?' Li shot him a hostile glance. The man lowered his eyes and fidgeted. Li had warned him on several occasions never to call her for any male visitor, unless the person looked as if he had come from the village. The security man had a reputation for making money through calling up girls for the rich Alhajis in town.

'A short man with a bushy face,' the security man winked. 'Never seen him here, you know. I like him,' he ended childishly.

'Of course you like all of them,' Li said to herself, 'provided they clasp your hand.' Meaning of course that they gave him money.

Aloud she asked once more, 'A short man with a bushy face? Who can that be?' The security man shrugged his shoulders. Li's eyes began to twitch again. She dropped her books and rushed past the security man.

'He is in the Camaru, Misi,' he shouted after her.

The man who had his back to the door swung round quickly as the common room door slammed. Still as a statue, he stood and stared at Li who had her back pressed against the door. For some few seconds they stared at each other.

Li was the first to speak. 'By God,' she stammered. 'By God, It's you—Sule.' She tottered towards her brother like a child learning his first steps. 'Where have you been?'

'By my ancestors,' Sule muttered, moving cautiously towards her. Inches away from each other, they stood silently, their eyes spanning the period of twelve years. Li's eyes were full of tears of happiness. Words eluded her, so she simply stared at the brother who was almost a stranger to her. Sule had changed, but so had she. Li supposed she could have passed him on the streets without recognising him, but then as the sages say, 'blood could recognise blood even in the dark.'

'Why, son-of-my-mother, what happened to your long legs?' Li teased her brother. 'You have grown short and extremely broad in the chest. Who indeed could have recognised you as the son-of-my-mother?'

And you, daughter-of-my-mother, I have to climb my mother's barn to look you in the face! Surely you have won the race for heights.'

'I did well for myself,' Li continued to tease him, 'but you, son-of-the-chief, must have been too busy planning mischief to grow into a proper man.'

'The gods, Li, they grew envious of me, but made you into a giant. Ye-ye-ye my ancestors,' he lamented mockingly. 'Upon all my woes, must I also have the new job of looking for a husband for my giant sister.' They broke into side-splitting laughter as they sat in the nearest chairs.

'You haven't changed a bit, son-of-my-mother,' Li said, wiping the tears from her eyes. 'Where have you been?' she asked for the second time.

'I cannot say the same about you, Li,' he studied his sister carefully. 'Even your laughter has gained some years.' Li simply looked into space.

'It is the way of the world,' she finally said. 'But you, you haven't done badly for yourself,' she looked at him with renewed interest.

'I struggled for years, Li. Many people would say I am now a successful businessman. But whatever I have acquired it tastes like ash. Home haunted me.'

'You are home now, Sule,' Li said. Sule nodded solemnly.

'You heard what happened then?' she asked fearfully, referring to their father's death.

'Not until yesterday.'

'So you just decided to come?' Li asked.

'Yes.'

They remained silent. Sule looked down at his boots that looked out of place in the common room. He studied the make of the chair he was sitting on and concluded the whole place looked too feminine for his liking. Li sniffed and he looked up. Tears were streaming down her face. 'Women's tears.' He was irritated. He could never understand why women cry. His wife's tears always drove him out of the house. He cracked his knuckles as he paced the room. The memories of his early years rushed over him in waves, but the memories had now lost their sting. He was no longer bitter, just sad.

Yes, sad. Sule felt he had a better reason to cry than Li. Years ago he had gone away with a curse on his head. Now that he felt responsible enough to handle his own affairs and ask for his father's pardon, he was told the man hadn't waited long enough for him to prove himself a worthy son. He cursed under his breath.

'How did you feel when you heard the news?' Li said,

interrupting his reverie.

'How should I feel, Li? After all, he was my father!' He sounded upset. 'I wish you had been reconciled before he died,' Li said passionately.

'It does not seem important any longer,' Sule said. 'Not after what I went through. I paid for what I did.'

'You suffered,' Li stated rather than questioned. 'Where have you been all these years?' she asked for the third time.

'I stole out of this country under a false name and without papers. For two years I travelled from one country to another under different names. As for jobs I have done everything —legal and illegal. I have been arrested more than once, but always acquitted. Now I wonder how I managed to escape a prison sentence.' He shook his head ruefully.

'The spirits of your ancestors were guiding you, son-of-my-mother.'

'I believe you, Li,' Sule answered. 'You would not believe the narrow escapes I've had and the lies I have told. One day, I'll tell you everything.' Sule lowered his head. 'God, I didn't know that even as I was weaving lies to save my own skin, my father lay silent in his grave. I only hope he pardoned me before the end,' Sule said.

'He did, Sule,' Li answered gently. 'He asked for you in his last hours.'

Suddenly Sule became alert. 'Did he say anything, Li.'

'No, he just wanted to see you. He too was in need of pardon, Sule,' Li said.

'May the spirits of his ancestors protect him,' Sule said. 'I should have come home after I was released. I had nowhere else to go. The officer in charge of the case pitied me and introduced me to a businessman friend of his. Together, they warned me that if I proved them wrong, I'd be shot without a trial.

'At first Alhaji Ahmadu, the businessman, wouldn't trust me. I used to sleep outside the house with the security man. But gradually I gained his confidence. Out of sheer gratitude, I devoted myself completely to my benefactor. I tried to wipe out my past in my work. He was pleasantly surprised to learn that I was literate and good at figures. He let me handle his accounts and his business prospered.

'Three times a year he sent me back to Nigeria to supervise his business in various cities. For six years we stayed together, during which time I built a small house and married his younger sister. Now I have two small girls.'

Li jumped for joy. 'Two small girls? Bring them home, son-of-my-mother.'

'Some day, Li, some day. Meanwhile I manage my master's business completely. He died last year.' He lowered his voice in grief.

'Assha!' Li exclaimed sympathetically 'Assha Sule, you have lost a friend.'

'He wasn't just a master and a brother-in-law, Li. He was like a father to me, the kind I never had before.'

Li nodded with understanding.

'After he died,' Sule continued, 'I felt empty once more. It was as if I had suddenly become rootless. The desire to come home turned into an obsession.' How could Sule now explain to Li that intense desire to go home? Years back, as he stamped off the dust of his home from his feet, he had vowed never to come back. But he had not reckoned with a force that was stronger than his vow. The cord that had tied him to his mother, had eventually pulled him back to his siblings. The siblings with whom he had shared the same womb and sucked the same breasts.

'I missed home badly,' he said simply. 'My wife understood and encouraged me to come. I was afraid, though. After all these years I didn't know what to expect. If I had thought of anyone dying, it was the two ancient ones. I contacted Garba in Kano. He told me everything I needed to know about everybody.'

He paused thoughtfully. 'My son, Li, how is he?'

'He is growing up well. The ancient one dotes on him,' Li replied. 'What did Garba say about Faku?,' she asked.

'That she deserted him and joined the gang of thousands of free women all over the country.'

'It's not true, Sule. Faku also had a dream, a deep need for security. She had grown up without a father — she yearned for a man's presence in her home. Any man that would claim relation with her. I remember her saying, and I can still see the glow on her face as she said it, "A man's muddy shoes outside my door! A man's commanding voice in the early hours of the day and the late hours of night. Where indeed is the Lord of the house who brings in food for his obedient wife to cook?" No, Sule, if any of us didn't mean to drift, it was Faku. She knew where she was going, but Garba could not understand. He failed to fill that vacuum in her life. I saw her, Sule, in her moments of dire need. She was uncomplaining but her whole body spoke of the hurt in her soul. I knew then she had to leave to survive!'

'I fear for Faku,' Sule replied. 'It is dangerous out there, daughter-of-my-mother. The experiences I had, taught me a lot of things about life. It softened my heart towards my father. I can now understand why he was obsessed with discipline. I could have ended up in prison, Li, but for the conscience my father instilled in me.'

Finally Li said, 'Are you coming home, Sule?'

'Home, Li? My home is in Niger. That is where my wife and children are.'

'But that is not your real home, big brother. What about us? There is no responsible man in the house. You are the most senior son.'

Sule shook his head sadly. 'Twelve years ago I vowed never to come, except as a visitor.'

'You cannot do that to us, son-of-my-mother. The home of your ancestors is here, not in Niger.'

'I am no longer sure, daughter-of-my-mother. I was born here, but the stranger country nurtured me to manhood, instilled in me a true sense of human values. It was there I understood the full meaning of independence.'

'I understand, Sule, but do not forget us. Do not forget that your umbilical cord was buried at the foot of your mother's barn. We shall be waiting for you to come and join hands in upholding the threshold of our ancestors.'

After a lengthy talk about old times, Sule left for the village. He was going to see the old people, his mother, his siblings and his son. From there he would return to his new country, Niger.

# Epilogue

'Li!' Awa's urgent voice pierced Li's thoughts. 'Li,' she repeated, coming in through the front double-doors of the large four-bedroomed house. 'Come out, Li,' Awa urged. 'The mourners are outside and waiting for you. You are the man of the house now.'

Li made no move. Awa stood before her and placed her hand on Li's shoulder. 'Dry your tears, daughter-of-my-mother. It is no time to cry. Tell the mourners how to bury the father of our father. He never went with the people of the book, nor was he ever known to have performed an ablution. But we have to honour him the best way we can, for he was a lion among men. A man without an equal, the last of his kind.'

'Call the drummers, big sister,' Li answered, wiping her face. 'Let them drink, beat drums and dance. Let them lay to rest the ghost of the father of my father, for he must be buried as he always lived, as a traditionalist.'

As the drums throbbed and the dancers sang the old man's praises and swung their hips in a drunken frenzy, the family converged in the largest room in the house. The children sat quietly in one corner. Most of them had no idea what had happened. Only a few of them remembered vaguely a day similar to this. The day Baba had died. But they all knew, from the wailing and crying in the early morning and the drunken singing and dancing this late afternoon that the previous night had robbed them of a devoted friend and father.

Li sat still in an armchair and crossed her elegant legs. At thirty-three, she looked years younger than her age. The trim waist-line and the unlined complexion were signs of careful cultivation, which belied years of fierce emotional struggle, and hard work. At last she had accomplished her ambitions. She was a successful teacher and an owner of a huge modern and enviable building. The rest of the huts had been demolished. Only two huts still stood. One had belonged to their grandmother who had died only a few months ago. The other one still held the corpse of the ancient one.

Li ought to have felt fulfilled, but instead she felt empty. It wasn't just the emptiness of bereavement, but an emptiness that went beyond that. For ten years she had struggled towards certain goals. Now, having accomplished these goals, she wished there was something else to struggle for. For that was the only way life could be meaningful.

She turned to her right and looked kindly at the occupant of the next chair. Li smiled and received a dimpled smile in return. Here was someone who had, at last, found a meaning in life. Li did not wonder at Faku's success, as she had never doubted her friend's sense of direction.

The previous day, Li had been overwhelmed with happiness when Faku had walked up and blindfolded her as they used to do when they were small. Then, Li would reach out for Faku's face to feel the dimples. But this time Awa came to her rescue with 'Eh! eh! eh! My ancestors, we have a visitor from the land of the dead. Faku, can this be you?' After that the house came to life. Everybody came out running, except the ancient one.

They had spent the whole afternoon chatting and today they were united in mourning. Yesterday, Li had listened spellbound to Faku's account of her experiences in various cities after finding the courage to leave Garba. For years, Faku had drifted without a proper sense of direction. Then, three years ago she had been befriended by a kind, elderly woman who interested herself in social welfare work. Now Faku was on the way to becoming a social welfare worker herself. Li felt happy for her friend who had found fulfilment at last.

She turned and watched her sister move her enormous size effortlessly. Years of constant hustling had made her steps light. She was everywhere at the same time. This was another person who had given her life for the happiness of others. Could she, Li, make some sort of an impact in her society?

Her mind went back to the previous night. It had been a trying one for both Li and Awa. Towards evening, after Faku had gone home, Awa went to the old man's hut to see if he needed anything. She had found him in a motionless heap besides the fire-hearth, his breathing laborious. She called Li and together they lifted him to a sitting position. He was in a bad way. Li sat with the old man, supporting his head on her thighs. Awa went to alert the neighbours. They came, but none could move Li from her position. She sat and talked to the ancient one while Awa fussed over her comfort. By midnight, everybody had dispersed, leaving the two sisters in their grandfather's hut. Mama also kept vigil in her own room. At the first cockrow, the old man passed away quietly. The women covered him with a blanket and retired to their rooms.

Now Li was tired. She wondered where Awa got her energy from. Her limbs ached from sitting still for a long time. Her thighs, where her grandfather's head had lain, felt like lead. She sighed and closed her eyes.

She was sitting by a fire-hearth warming her aching limbs. Supporting her chin with the palm of her hand and resting the elbow on her withered thigh, Li stared into the fire thoughtfully. Someone stole into the room, the footsteps almost inaudible. Li felt rather than saw the presence. The person came close to her and stood behind the stool. Li raised her fading eyes with difficulty and saw an amazing sight which puzzled her. A young girl of about twenty stood there, tall and graceful, her skin ebony black. A smile revealed a beautiful gap between the upper row of teeth. The girl bent down and peered closely into Li's eyes.

'Great-grandmother,' the girl called. 'You have been sitting here for hours. Everybody is in the courtyard performing the marriage rites.'

'Is that so, child?' Li asked weakly.

'It is even so, great-grandmother, and we are waiting for you to bless the occasion. A lot of people are here only to see you.'

'What occasion?' Li asked absentmindedly.

'My marriage, great-grandmother! Have you forgotten I am getting married today?'

'No, child, it is fresh in my mind,' Li replied, sleepily.

'Then come, ancient one. Our husband swears you are the best wife,' the girl said mischievously. 'Come, let me show you off to my guests.'

She raised Li's hand to her cheeks. With a shock Li observed how withered her hands were. She removed her hand from the girl's grip.

'No child.' She shook her head sadly. 'This time it is your dream. Go and make the best of it. Don't be like me. I spent my entire life dreaming, I forgot to live.'

'No, great-grandmother! It isn't true. You were a success, remember? You gave your life for the welfare of the people.'

'It is well to dream, child,' she went on as if she hadn't heard the girl. 'Everybody does, and as long as we live, we shall continue to dream. But it is also important to remember that like babies dreams are conceived but not all dreams are born alive. Some are aborted. Others are stillborn.'

'Great-grandmother,' the girl wailed, 'are you dreaming now?'

'No, child. It is just that I realised too late that her arms were longer than mine.'

'Whose arms, great-grandmother?' the girl asked in alarm.

'Fate, child. The arm of fate struck my baby in the womb,' Li said sadly.

The young girl shook her head. She thought the ancient one was muddled in her mind. 'By God, old age must be a terrible thing,' she said almost to herself. Raising her voice she said, 'Get up, co-mate. Go to bed. You cannot stay alone much longer.'

'I am not alone,' she said sharply. 'I have never been alone. I have Habu Adams.'

'Habu Adams?' The girl was thoroughly amused now. 'By God, my late great-grandfather!' She giggled, looking round to see if there was anybody around to share in the amusement.

'You are tired, great grand-mother. Get up or I will carry you to bed.'

Li felt a firm grip on her shoulder and woke up with a start. Shuwa, her ten-year-old daughter, had her hand on Li's shoulder and was laughing into her face. 'Were you dreaming about my father, mama?' she asked.

Li felt embarrassed. She quickly looked up and met Awa's steady eyes across the room. So the girl knew her father's name? It was just as well. In a few seconds, Li had gone fifty or more years into the future. She knew now that the bond that had tied her to the father of her child was not ruptured. And in spite of everything, in the soft cradle of her heart, there was another baby forming. This time Li was determined the baby would not be stillborn.

'Big sister,' Li called.

'Uhmm?' Awa raised her head.

'I am going back to the city,' she said simply.

'To the city, Li?' Awa asked in surprise.

'Yes, to the city. And I am taking Shuwa with me,' she said firmly.

Awa shook her head thoughtfully. 'You are going back to him?'

'Yes.'

'Why, Li? The man is lame,' said the sister.

'We are all lame, daughter-of-my-mother. But this is no time to crawl. It is time to learn to walk again.'

'So you want to hold the crutches and lead the way?' Awa asked.

'No,' answered Li.

'What then, you want to walk behind and arrest his fall?'

'No. I will just hand him the crutches and side by side we will learn to walk.'

'May the gods of your ancestors guide you,' Awa said.

'May the good God guide us all,' replied Li.

# Behind the Clouds

Ifeoma Okoye

Ije and Dozie Apia are a young Nigerian couple who seem to have everything: wordly success, material prosperity, and an unusually close and loving relationship. There is only one cloud on their horizon: they have no child.

Ije has tried everything, undergone tests and examinations, swallowed potions, consulted herbalists and faith-healers. Her mother-in-law reviles her as a failure and urges her son to take another wife. Secure in Dozie's love, Ije never for a moment dreams that such a thing could happen.

But then the nightmare begins . . . the nightmare from which it seems there is no escape.

Ifeoma Okoye has written a moving story about a human situation with which all African women will sympathise.

Drumbeat 58
ISBN 0 582 78555 3